A Quiet Place to Die

Simon Quellen Field

A Quiet Place to Die

Cover art by Simon Quellen Field

Published by MicroScience Press

19395 Montevina Road

Los Gatos, California, 95033

www.scitoys.com

ISBN 978-0-9822104-2-0

First edition: December 2008

Second edition: February 2023

To Kathleen, my muse.

The Lecher of County Kildare

They tell hereabouts, over ales and strong stouts,
of the young lady Molly McDear,
Who came from afar, to tend to the bar,
and pour all the laddies their beer.

She came into town, and walked all around,
to find out what lodging was there,
But because of the boom, t'only one who had rooms,
was the Lecher of County Kildare.

She didn't think twice, she thought he was nice,
and the price was no burden at all,
For the town was ablaze in those heady old days
 and the tipping was good at the hall.

But as time went along, and those good jobs were gone,
and the factory closed in oh eight,
Poor Molly McDear couldn't pour enough beer
 to prevent the month's rent being late.

She was up in a bind, but the landlord was kind,
and he made her an offer quite fair,
If you owe me a bit, you can show me a (bit),
and the books will be tidy and square.

So it went for some years, when she got in arrears,
he would always be gentle and kind,
If you owe me two bits, you can show me your (bits),
and the ledger will balance just fine.

No longer young maid, fewer tips she was paid,
and her debt grew the tab she had run,
If you owe me a lot, you can (show) me a lot,
and the record is settled and done.

For years it went on, and her youth it was gone,
and her dollars were down to just one,
If you owe me a buck, you can give me a (luck),
and the balance that's due will be none.

The two of them cared, under roof that they shared,
for the other as much for the fun,
Miss Molly, he said, I would like to be wed,
and forever for me you're the one.

I would love to my dear, I've lived happily here,
in your house for near half of my life,
You have been such a gent, but you must raise the rent,
if you're going to make me your wife

Jimmy Davis

I knew better than to answer the phone. The ring tone was the cackle of the wicked witch of the west, so I knew it was my ex-wife Silvia calling my cell phone.

The early morning waves slapped gently at the bow of my little sailboat, anchored in the cove at Moss Landing, one of the few possessions I escaped with from that marriage. The other major possession was the small house my mother had left me, on whose small rental income I now survived, when not writing the occasional insignificant local color pieces for small newspapers.

I knew better, but I answered it anyway. I'm a sucker. I know.

"Hi Jimmy," she said. It was not in the tone she used in the divorce court. It was not in the tone she used when we had dated, back when I was a detective. She had been running the Western Region investigations division for a large insurance company I no longer wanted to do business with. This was the tone she used when she wanted me to do something for her. Usually something unpleasant.

"Hi yourself," I said, sitting up in the small bunk and banging my head on the low ceiling again, as I did at least daily. The boat rocked, and the slap of the waves at the bow got louder as the wake of a passing boat told me it was past breakfast time.

"I need you to do a big favor for me," she said.

I let her breath into the phone a few times before I answered. "Why would I want to do that?" I asked.

"It's a job. Big money on this one, and a nice per diem, too. Up on the north coast."

A job. I could think of nothing I needed less right now. I was out of the kind of business she was offering anyway. I liked being out of it.

"Don't you have people for that? I thought Lee Aleada handled things for you north of Frisco," I said. She hated it when I called it Frisco. So now I never call it anything else, when she's around. Not that she was ever around.

"That's why the money is big, Jimmy. It's one of our own. Lee was shot and killed up in Russian Cove, on a simple assignment, checking out a possible suicide. Now it looks like a probable homicide, given that someone thought Lee was getting too close. I don't have anyone I can spare, and no one as good as you anyway."

I'm a sucker for flattery. But I was not biting. Besides, Lee Aleada had been an asshole and a bully. Nobody liked him. "What do the locals have on it?" I asked.

"The sheriff's department sent someone out to look around and take names, but it's been almost two weeks and they have squat. This one could really use the Jimmy Davis touch, Jimmy. Someone without a badge, who can get cozy with the locals, get someone to talk."

Or get shot.

"And end up like Lee? Are you trying to get rid of me, darling?" I asked.

She ignored the sarcastic endearment.

"I did that two years ago. This is business, Jimmy. You knew Lee. His wife is calling me every day. I need you on this one."

I never could deny her anything. That's why she got the big house, and I got the boat. I knew when I picked up the phone I would say yes. But I stretched it out as far as I could.

A Quiet Place to Die

"Send me what you have," I said. "I'll take a look, but no promises. And double the per diem. I'm not taking the boat up there."

"Thank you, Jimmy. I knew, I mean, just thank you," she said. "I'll email you all I have. Take care."

I disconnected without saying anything. I probably would have said something stupid.

I put on a T-shirt and a pair of sweat pants, and rowed the little dinghy in to the marina, where I could take a hot shower and get some breakfast not cooked by an amateur. When I felt a little more human, I rowed back to the boat, and got out the laptop computer and plugged it into the cell phone.

I had a lot of mail to catch up on. I ignored most of it, and pulled up the one from Silvia. There were several large attachments that took a while to download over the phone, despite the claims of high-speed broadband. Out on the water, you get what you get.

I scanned the documents quickly, looking for the meat. Lee Aleada had been sent out to determine whether the asphyxiation death of one Daniel McDougal was a suicide. McDougal had been found in his 1972 VW Beetle, wedged against the guardrail above a 200-foot drop to the rocky surf below. The car had scraped the guardrail for over 40 feet, apparently at low speed.

McDougal had no marks on him, there were no signs of a struggle, and no means of asphyxiation was discovered. In the car was a wrapped present, containing a stuffed teddy bear, and an empty cardboard box, damp from the rain. The windows were all up, and the heater was set to recirculate, but there was no way even the notoriously airtight Beetle could have caused the suffocation of the driver.

Aleada had spent four days in Russian Cove, interviewing anyone he could find. He sent daily email reports to Silvia, which I transferred to the phone for later reading. It would take most of the day to get from Moss Landing to Russian Cove, and I would need to get started soon. I checked Silvia's letter. The per diem was $1600. I decided to call a limousine service.

McDougal had owned a tavern and bed and breakfast. That made the accommodations decision easy. I looked through my wardrobe for something suitable to stuff into a duffle, but living small had made the selection meager, and laundry day was overdue. I decided the $1600 would cover clothing and luggage, and I swapped the sweatpants for Levi's and put on a pair of sneakers. Rowing back to shore, I looped the cable lock through the mooring cleat, and carried the oars into the marina office.

I chatted with Maria in the office while I waited for the limo to arrive. She'd watch the boat, and the dinghy, and the oars could stay propped in the corner until I returned. The limo arrived and took me into town, waited while I shopped, and the driver helped me stow my new luggage in the trunk. Then we were off, and I disappointed the driver by spending the trip reading Lee Aleada's reports on the tiny screen of my phone, using my strongest pair of cheap reading glasses. The reading went slowly, as I had to stop frequently to avoid motion sickness, something I, as a newly minted sailor, felt no small shame about.

Daniel McDougal, Danny to everyone in Russian Gulch, had gotten into a one-sided fistfight the night he died. A drunken patron of the tavern, apparently a regular, had taken offense at the notion that he had more than enough to drink that evening. Danny had apparently decked him after dodging a wild swing in his direction. Rafael Gonzales, Rafe to his friends, was particularly maudlin at the wake, and seemed to regret that his last words to his host had been indiscrete.

There were several pages on a man named Gill Barnett. Aleada had been having trouble getting Barnett's whereabouts verified, and apparently, Barnett was not very good at fabricating alibis. Three different versions of his activities on the night of McDougal's death were found to be false, one by one, and Aleada had marked this as needing follow-up.

I looked up as the limousine hit a bump. We were on the freeway, and traffic was surprisingly light. I went back to my reading.

Gonzales, Barnett, and another man, John McCarthy (known as Johnny Mac locally) were commercial fishermen who were regulars at McDougal's tavern. Aleada had followed McCarthy far south, to a small town where he spent a lot of time with a man named Hack Hartley, who ran a gay bar and was apparently very fond of McCarthy. Aleada had notes from discussions with several bar patrons, who referred to the couple as Mac 'n Hack. This relationship was apparently kept quite secret from his drinking buddies in Russian Gulch, and his fellow fishermen.

By the time we got to Sonoma County and onto the coast highway, my head was swimming with too much detail, and the winding road made it impossible to read. The headache was combining with the nausea, and I was mentally trying to find ways to blame all of this on Silvia.

The high cliffs over the crashing surf on the rocks below might have been scenic under other circumstances, but all I could think of at the moment was that crashing through the guardrail would bring the trip to a merciful end right away. It didn't help that the road kept going up hills and down, in addition to winding along the coast.

Listen to yourself, I thought. Complaining about a headache. Can't handle a ride in a limousine. I felt the shoulder where the bullet had shattered through bone and come out the other side. That was pain. A year of surgery after surgery, painful physical therapy, and two years living with a left arm that would never be what it used to be. What was a headache to that?

It was the bullet that shattered my life, as it had shattered bones and ligaments. The cocky, fearless detective, so sure of himself, so good at what he did. That was gone. With it went the job I no longer wanted to do, the wife, the house, the self-respect. Look at me now, whining because the road was winding. Silvia was expecting that old Jimmy Davis. This new one, what was he doing here, playing investigator?

The sun was about to set over the ocean when we finally reached Russian Cove. The driver crept past several small, well-spaced houses until he found McDougal's, and stopped the car. I got out, and spent a few minutes getting my legs to work again while the driver got my luggage from the trunk and carried it inside. I pulled out a sizeable tip from my wallet, and hoped that it would make his trip back alone in the dark a little happier.

I hadn't expected McDougal's to be so large. The buildings were set back from the road quite a bit, and a slate path wound around fishponds and over a small wooden bridge to two enormous wooden doors with wrought iron handles. Something moved in the corner of my eye, and I turned to watch a mother raccoon shepherding several cubs into the shadows.

My luggage was arrayed neatly in the front office, but there was no one at the desk. Alone in the room, I looked up at the high wooden ceilings, and more of the wrought ironwork that seemed to be the architect's favorite motif. From the building to my right, I could hear the slightly muffled sounds of a live band, playing what might have been fast Irish folk music.

My driver accepted the tip without counting it, and left me alone in the big room. Reckoning that my luggage would be safe unattended for a few minutes, I followed the sound of the music into the tavern section of the estate. Opening another ten-foot high door made of thick pine planks bound with iron, the noise level rose immediately to a level that would make conversation impossible.

A Quiet Place to Die

The band played on a stage at the far end of the room. Below the stage was a large group of roughly dressed men, probably commercial fishermen just off their boats, having a pint before making their way home. They were loudly singing along with the band. A petite redhead played a pennywhistle when she wasn't singing, and she was backed up by a man playing a huge string bass, a drummer, a guitarist, and an accordion player. The redhead danced as she sang, twirling a short skirt and teasing the noisy crowd below.

To my left was a long polished hardwood bar, at which sat several patrons on stools. In the center of the room were several round tables, mostly occupied with a slightly better dressed clientele, which I took to be guests of the lodge. I walked over to an open spot at the bar, and attracted the attention of the barmaid.

"What are you having?" she shouted over the din.

"I booked a room this morning," I shouted back. "I just arrived, and there's no one in the office."

She grabbed a towel and wiped her hands, then lifted the bar gate and stepped over to my side of the bar. I followed her back out the door into the office. As the big door swung shut behind us, the noise level dropped to a whisper, and I could hear my ears ringing.

"Sorry about that. We're a bit shorthanded," she said, moving to the computer. Her fingers moved over the keys for a bit, and then she said, "You're Mr. Davis?"

I nodded. She picked out a key, and stepped out next to me, picking up two of my suitcases. I took the heavier one from her, picked up the last, and followed her out to the slate path with the fishponds.

"Yours is upstairs on the right," she said. "Number 203 has a great view of the ocean from the back, and the hills from the front. Wood for the fireplace is at the end of the building in case you run out, but we bring a fresh bundle to your room during housekeeping.

Breakfast is anything from seven to ten in the morning. Let us know if you have any special dietary needs." She sounded like she was reciting from memory. Like this long a speech was unusual for her.

We walked up the stairs, past rooms 201 and 202, and she put her key in the lock.

"There's a high speed network port at the table behind the Jacuzzi, but there's also wireless."

The room was large and warm, and far enough away from the tavern that even with the door open, the music was just a whisper.

"Very nice," I said. "I write stories for local newspapers about special places and events," I said, establishing a cover that would be at once innocuous but would also give me an excuse for being nosy. "Is there anything special planned nearby for the week? Or for Halloween perhaps? I did a great feature piece last year of a little girl's first trip to the Half Moon Bay Art and Pumpkin festival." That part was true, except for the part about it being great. Got me a hundred bucks, though.

"There's a calendar in the office with all the local stuff," she said. "Have a nice stay, Mr. Davis."

"Call me Jimmy. And you are?"

"Abby," she said.

"Abby who?" I prompted.

"McDougal. I own this place. As of September 29th."

I was going to pump some more, but I stopped. I could not figure out a way to pry past that statement without violating my own sense of decency. I could pretend to be ignorant, I *would* pretend to be ignorant, but I would have to find a gentle way to get her to talk about that. Besides, she was hardly going to confide in some guest she'd just met.

She was about to leave when I stopped her. "Do you have some aspirin? I have a terrible headache. Tried to do some reading in the back seat on the drive up. Big mistake."

"We have some in the office. I'll have some brought up."

"Oh, no bother, I'll come down. I want to check out your local nightlife anyway. It looks like quite a crowd in the bar tonight," I said, trying to be chatty.

"Not as bad as Fridays," she said, handing me the key and closing the door behind us. We walked back to the office. "Oh, and don't feed the raccoons. They'll bite your hand off."

In the office, she found a bottle of aspirin and handed it to me. "I'll get you a glass of water from the bar," she said, leading the way towards the noise. She opened the big doors and once again, the wall of noise assaulted me.

The lead singer was dancing quickly, spinning and stomping her feet to the music as she played her pennywhistle. The tune was fast and melodic, and the crowd up by the stage was stomping along with her. I followed Abigail McDougal to the bar, and she raised the gate and slipped under quickly, and with professional speed filled a glass of water for me, slid it to me over the bar, and put all her attention to the other customers, trying to make up the time she had lost checking me in.

The singer lowered her whistle and leaned into the microphone.

> *She came into town, and walked all around, to find out what lodging was there,*
> *But because of the boom, t'only one who had rooms, was the Lecher of County Kildare.*

The crowd below her sang along loudly, making it difficult to hear some of the words.

> *She didn't think twice, she thought he was nice, and the price was no burden at all,*
> *For the town was ablaze in those heady old days, and the tipping was good at the hall.*

I scanned the room again. Most of the rowdy group seemed to know the words, while the people at the tables watched the flamboyant singer stomp and spin. Most of the customers at the bar were also watching, as there was little point in trying to make conversation.

> *But as time went along, and those good jobs were gone, and the factory closed in oh eight,*
> *Poor Molly McDear couldn't pour enough beer, to prevent the month's rent being late.*

> *She was up in a bind, but the landlord was kind, and he made her an offer quite fair,*
> *If you owe me a bit, you can show me a (bit), and the books will be tidy and square.*

It was hard to make out exactly what the singer had said, because half the room shouted that one word, whether they had been singing along or not. I decided this was one of the bawdier Irish folk songs, and the singer was using polite words while the drunks were not.

> *So it went for some years, when she got in arrears, he would always be gentle and kind,*
> *If you owe me two bits, you can show me your (bits), and the ledger will balance just fine.*

At this point, the singer bowed deeply to the crowd below, giving them a good view of the ample cleavage her well-engineered brassiere provided. The crowd roared their appreciation, and the stomping got even louder. The singer brought up her pennywhistle again, and played the melody with three grace notes for every note, fingers dancing along the whistle holes faster than the eye could follow.

Several more bawdy verses went by, and my headache was not getting any better, despite the aspirin. The noise in the room, and perhaps the warm air, were not doing me any good. The tempo of the music slowed, and the drunks got quiet.

> *The two of them cared, under roof that they shared, for the other as much for the fun,*
> *Miss Molly, he said, I would like to be wed, and forever for me you're the one.*
>
> *I would love to my dear, I've lived happily here, in your house for near half of my life,*
> *You have been such a gent, but you must raise the rent, if you're going to make me your wife.*

The tempo jumped quickly back, and the singer brought the pennywhistle up to her mouth again, and raced the band to the finish with a flourish, stomping and spinning, until I thought the whole room would keel over in a faint trying to help her breathe. Finally, the last note crashed into a cymbal and the song came to an end. A shout came up from the group under the stage, as the singer bowed low again.

"Thank you! Thank you! We're Pennywhistle, and we'll be playing here all week. Don't forget the tip jar at the front of the stage, and the tip jar for Molly at the bar. We're going to take a short break, and be back with more real soon."

The singer jumped from the stage and skipped over to the bar, where Abigail McDougal was ready with a tall glass of water. As she drained the glass in one long tip, swallow after swallow, Abigail waited. When the singer had finished, I could hear Abigail shout.

"Where's Gill tonight?"

The singer flung a rude gesture in no particular direction, and shouted back "Who the fuck cares!"

I saw Abigail raise her eyebrow at that, and the singer went back to the stage, and picked up a conversation with the band. Abigail took the glass away, but continued to watch the singer. She only broke away when a new customer came up to the bar.

Mentally judging the size of the crowd, I wondered what the odds were of there being two people named Gill in the room, and whether the Gill being discussed was the same Gill Barnett that Lee Aleada had suspicions about. I'm not a math whiz. I decided the odds were against coincidence. They usually are.

It would be no surprise that the two women would know the regular customer. But Abigail seemed to think that the singer would know his whereabouts this night, and that was something to explore. But not tonight. My head was pounding, and I had a phone call to make before I tried to sleep it away.

I left the crowded tavern, and when the big door swung shut behind me, my ears felt like they were under pillows. Everything seemed quiet and muffled. I made my way up the stairs to room 203, and stood on the boardwalk in front of the room for a moment, looking around the grounds from my high perch. The raccoons were fishing in one of the ponds, and I could hear the occasional quiet rush of a passing car on the highway, blending in with the sounds of surf on the rocks far away and down the cliffs, and the faint buzz of the tavern. I turned the key in the lock and entered the room.

The heaviest of my suitcases held the laptop computer, my gun and shoulder holster, binoculars, camera, various lenses, and other assorted tools of the trade, cushioned by some of my new clothing. I brought out the computer, and plugged the charger into the wall behind the desk.

I pulled out my cell phone to make the call, but decided to use the room phone instead. I looked up the sheriff's number in Aleada's notes, and called.

"Sheriff's department," a man's voice answered.

"Is the sheriff available?" I asked.

"Not at this hour. Can I help you?"

"My name is Jimmy Davis. I'm here in Russian Cove, staying at McDougal's, on behalf of Silvia Porter, with whom the sheriff should be familiar. I'm here investigating the affair with Daniel McDougal and Lee Aleada, for the company. Tell the sheriff I called as a courtesy, and I will be in tomorrow, at his convenience, for a meeting face to face. I look forward to cooperating with the department."

"Ok, just a sec. Who did you say you were?"

"Jimmy Davis. I'm working for Silvia Porter on the McDougal and Aleada investigations."

"Porter...Alley Ada. Ok, I'll make sure he gets this."

"Thank you," I said, and put down the phone.

The bed was firm, the sheets were cool, and my head throbbed as I lay down. The notes of the pennywhistle played in my head until I was finally able to doze off.

§

Gabe Corcoran

Blue jays at my window woke me early the next day, just before dawn. I sat up quickly. Somewhat surprised that I didn't smack my head on a low ceiling, I remembered where I was. The window facing the hills showed a cloudless pale blue sky, and the hills themselves were glowing at the edges with the pre-dawn backlight of the sun.

By the time I'd showered and dressed, the sun was peeking over the hills to the east, and I stepped out into the cool breeze of an October morning. From the upstairs walkway outside my door, I could see whitecaps out past the kelp, and pelicans perched on the rocks watching the surf.

I walked down the stairs and over to the main office. Once again, there was no one there. However, a small handwritten sign taped to the counter read "Breakfast". An arrow under the word pointed to the left, opposite where the band had played the night before, where another pair of the ten-foot high doors was propped open.

I followed the arrow, and walked into a large, high ceilinged room with small tables clustered at one end, and a huge table at the other, covered with a white tablecloth, and set with plates for breakfast. An older couple was sitting at the large table, near the center, and they waved me over.

"Hi there," I said as I approached. "I'm Jimmy Davis."

"Isn't it a fine morning?" the woman said. "I'm Gina Franco. This is my husband, George." The man stood and reached to shake my hand. His grip was much too strong for comfort, and I let him squeeze my hand painfully until he felt satisfied. I pretended not to feel injured, sure that if I had tried to squeeze back he would only have pressed the issue. I wasn't here to compete.

"We're the early birds," George said, sitting back down. "Most of the other guests make it down around eight or nine. Me, I can't see the point of staying in bed half the day when you're here to enjoy a nice change of pace."

A Quiet Place to Die

He was a large man in bulk, build, and height. He had black hair shot through with strands of steel gray, and a mustache that looked like a large caterpillar had taken up residence on his upper lip.

"I'd guess those who closed down the party last night probably need their beauty rest," I said. "I might have joined them, but I had a terrible headache last night, and turned in early. Have you been here long? I don't mean this morning. I mean have you met many of our fellow guests?"

Gina was also rather plump, with an enormous bosom whose cleavage could have hidden any number of useful items, or the better portion of last night's dinner.

"We've been here since Friday night," she said. "There's a young couple who got in about noon on Saturday, and two young men here to go abalone diving, they got here yesterday. Gosh, it's Tuesday already, half our week is up almost."

George put down his coffee cup. "There's that old guy in the hat, Randy something. He's a photographer, likes to come up this time of year to take pictures of the waves and stuff. We come up here every year, and he's been here the last three years running. Spends a month or so, hauling his tripod and that huge camera around everywhere he goes."

When George took a breath, Gina filled in the brief pause. "And lately, you know, there's been that sheriff's deputy. You heard about that fellow that was shot down at the RV park? That happened the same night we got here. He was staying here at the lodge! That deputy parked his car right outside our window and all night long that radio kept squawking and I hardly got a wink of sleep."

I made a surprised face. "One of the guests was shot?"

"Oh yes," Gina said, eager to spread the news to a new ear. "They say he was here investigating Mr. McDougal's accident. He's the owner of the lodge. We used to have breakfast with him every year. He ran off the road just a couple weeks ago, I think it was a heart attack, they say he didn't have a scratch on him, and he was so old, you know. He used to greet all the guests, fix breakfast, and handle all the running of the lodge. Now little Abigail has to do everything herself. That's his daughter. She used to just tend the bar. I don't know if she's cut out for doing it all by herself, she should get some help. You know — someone who's good with people. Maybe she's still upset, poor dear, but she's just not a people person, you know what I mean?"

I nodded, and smiled as George made an apologetic face, careful not to let his wife see.

"So, Mr. Davis," George said, "What do you do for a living? I'm in construction, Franco Builders, in San Jose. Mostly commercial stuff, but some residential. What are you getting away from?"

I smiled again. "Call me Jimmy," I said. "I'm a freelance writer, mostly local color travel pieces for small newspapers. Stuff that sells real estate ads, you know what I mean. So I get to pretend I'm here on business. I get to write it off on my taxes if I do some little piece on the lodge or the scenery."

Abigail McDougal came out from a door that must have led to the kitchen, saving me any more elaboration.

"Would you like some coffee? I can bring your breakfast if you like, or are you waiting for some more guests?"

"Coffee would be great," I said. "And there's no rush, we can wait for some more guests to fill out the table. Unless George and Gina are hungry?" I looked at my tablemates.

"Let's see who shows up in the next half hour," George said. "But if it's much longer than that, screw 'em."

"George!" said Gina, hitting him gently on the shoulder.

"I'll be back with that coffee," Abby said. She went back into the kitchen.

"See what I mean?" Gina said quietly, leaning across the table, almost whispering. "She's going about her business like nothing happened at all. I don't understand the Irish. They had a big party instead of a funeral. Everybody was drunk, and there was music and everything. That was all before we got here, you know, but I heard all about it from that Spanish girl who does the beds in the morning."

"She's Mexican," George corrected. "She just speaks Spanish."

"She speaks English. It's just hard to tell what she's saying. I have to listen really hard. She said they scattered his ashes in the ocean, and then they all came back and had a big party, and everybody got really drunk and they stayed up all night, and there was music and dancing. Imagine, dancing at a funeral! And then the next day she's showing guests to their rooms just like he used to do, except she never smiles, not once. But I looked in her eyes, you know, to see if she cries at night, you know, and there's nothing there, no red, just plain eyes. She doesn't wear mascara, so I can't tell if it runs, you know, so who knows?"

She sat back up in her chair as Abby brought out my coffee. I smiled up at her, and took the cup and saucer out of her hands before she could set it down. "That smells great," I said, smiling broadly. She nodded, and headed back into the kitchen. I was going to have to work on Abby if I was going to get her to open up and talk to me.

I took a sip of the coffee black, and decided to add cream and sugar to make it palatable. I had seen a cappuccino machine in the bar — this coffee had not come from there.

Gina looked up at someone behind me, and I turned to see a gray bearded man in a crushable fishing hat coming up to the table. He nodded at me, and took the seat next to mine.

"Jimmy Davis," I said, extending a hand.

"Randy Hanson," he said, taking my hand much gentler than George Franco had.

"George was just telling me about a photographer staying with us, is that you?" I asked.

"You should see the size of that thing he carries around," George said. "Like a cannon."

"Actually, it's a Nikon," Randy said. I smiled.

"I'm a freelance journalist," I said. "I take some shots for stories sometimes. Maybe you could point me at some of the best places for nice travel shots, something I could write a piece around?"

"You here covering the shooting?" he asked.

"No, not my kind of thing, I just heard about it this morning. I do local color, travel stuff, nothing heavy."

"Stuff that sells real estate," George explained.

I nodded. "But you were here when that happened, right?" I said. "Did you know the guy? I heard he was a guest here."

"Lee. Yeah, he was here for four days, snooping around a lot, bothering the locals. He worked for some insurance company, seemed to think there was something wrong with the way Danny died. He spooked a lot of people. Nobody wanted to talk to him after a while. He had a way of looking at people, like everybody was guilty of something."

Hanson looked around for a coffee cup, but didn't find one.

"The deputy thinks someone from the lodge did the shooting," he continued. "The gun was Danny's — someone took it from the box behind the bar, where all of the stuff from his car got stowed, after the accident. I think that's nuts. I know these people. None of them would shoot someone. They're all just simple people, making a living. I think some rowdy from up north stole the gun out of the box and tried to rob the guy. Everybody knew the gun was in there. It was in there for two whole weeks, and there were hundreds of people in the bar during that time."

"Someone from up north?" I asked. This had not been in Silvia's email.

"Yeah, from Pine Grove, or Caspar. There are biker bars up there, and those guys come through here on their way to San Fran, nothing but trouble. I hear a Harley coming; I pack up the gear in the trunk."

Gina again looked over my shoulder and I turned to see a young couple entering the room. Gina waved; probably glad to have a reason to change the subject. She leaned over to me and whispered. "I'd introduce you, but I swear I have totally forgotten their names."

"No problem," I said. I stood up as they joined us, and held out my hand. "Jimmy Davis," I said.

The man shook my hand briefly and said "Dave Hartley. This is my wife Janet." She waited while he pulled a chair out for her. I wondered if George was ever that old-fashioned or romantic. Or if Janet had insisted on teaching Dave. I smiled, as it seemed so much like something from an old movie. Then again, I was divorced. Maybe I could learn something.

"Jimmy writes stories for newspapers," George said.

"I read one of those once," Hartley said. "They had those before the Internet, right?"

"That's me," I said. "Fred Flintstone in the age of the Jetsons. Gina and Randy were just filling me in on all the excitement going on here in the last couple of weeks. You here for the quiet romantic vacation spot?"

"Janet is here studying kelp forest ecology. I paint, so I can work anywhere. I'm doing a lot of sketches of cliffs and rocks right now, trying to ignore all the scuba gear strewn about."

I got little else of any interest out of the group during breakfast, and I had not heard back from the sheriff's office, despite checking my cell phone several times to see if it was still working properly. I excused myself at the earliest opportunity, and went back to my room.

"Sheriff's office," said a woman's voice over the phone. I explained who I was again, and asked when I could see the deputy handling the Aleada investigation.

"He's down where you are, checking out a missing person report. If he's not at McDougal's yet, he will be soon, I'd bet. You can't miss the car. It's got Corcoran for Sheriff pasted all over it."

I thanked her, and closed the phone. From my doorway, I could see the front parking lot, but no cars had political signage. I could not see the rear bumpers, however, so I went down the stairs to get a closer look at the cars.

One of the nice things about using the freelance writer cover is that you get to carry a notebook around and take notes. But it is even easier to carry a pocket camera with you for things like remembering license plate numbers. In the parking lot, it was easy to get a shot of all of the cars in the lot, under the pretext of getting a good tourist photo of the lodge itself.

I had just taken a couple of shots when Corcoran's car pulled into the parking lot. It was indeed festooned with magnetic campaign signs. Unmarked except for an unused blue and red flashing light on the dash for pulling over speeders, the light blue station wagon was in need of a wash and some touch-up paint.

Corcoran had some difficulty getting out of the car. A portly man, he was perhaps a few inches taller than five feet, and the seat was pulled close to the steering wheel. The array of items attached to his belt caught in the wheel, the doorframe, and the seat belt, and he was not the picture of grace exiting the vehicle.

"Deputy Sheriff Corcoran, I presume," I said, walking up to the car. "Jimmy Davis," I said, extending a hand. "I called your office yesterday. I'm here working for Silvia Porter, although I'd prefer to keep that information just between the two of us for the moment, to make my investigation a little easier."

He looked at me the way he might have looked at the bottom of his shoe after stepping in something unpleasant. "That bitch just doesn't give up. Calls every day, as if we don't have important things to do. Now you. There's an election in exactly three weeks from today. So unless you're registered to vote in this county, and I expect you're not, I won't be much worried about making your life easier."

This was not someone who worried about first impressions.

"Nice to meet you too," I said, putting on a big smile. "My job is all about making your life easier. I'd like nothing more than to help you catch the bad guys, hopefully well before November 4th, and crawl back under my rock and leave all the applause for our elected officials. I'm here as a newspaper reporter as far as anyone but yourself knows, and I'd love to keep that fiction up, and leave the public relations part up to your department. I'm hired help, with someone else paying the bill. People will talk to me in a way they don't talk to official investigators, and you may find that helpful."

Corcoran was facing the lodge, not looking at me as I spoke. He half turned his head towards me when I finished, and regarded me out of the corner of his eye. "You don't put off easy, *do* you?" he said. He began walking towards the lodge, adjusting his laden belt under his considerable paunch. I followed.

He briefly glanced at the empty reception area as we entered the lodge, and turned right towards the bar without breaking his stride. He opened the tall heavy door and stepped in, ignoring me. I grabbed the door as it started to shut, and followed him in.

Abby McDougal was pulling chairs down off the tables, where they had been stored upside down while the floor had been vacuumed. Her hair was slightly disarranged, wisps at the sides having pulled out from her ponytail.

"Hi Gabe," she said to the deputy, as she smoothed out the tablecloth. "What is it this time?" She did not stop for the greeting, but continued to pull down chairs and arrange them at the table.

"Catherine Barnett says Gill didn't come home last night. He also didn't make it onto the boat in the morning. We found his car over at Pelican Point, all locked up, nobody around."

"So you're Cathy Barnett's errand boy, because her daddy is financing your campaign? Isn't it a little early to call in the cops when a guy is sleeping off a hangover under a rock somewhere?" Abby did not look up as she spoke, and went to the next table and pulled down another chair.

"Come on, Abby. She's worried. He comes here every night for a beer after work, and every night he's home in bed by eleven o'clock. He takes the kids to school in the morning. Now he's missing, no phone calls to home, to the guys on his boat, and his car is sitting out on the point, five miles from home. All I want to know from you is was he here last night, and was there anything odd going on. Can you tell me that, Abby?"

Abby stopped adjusting the tablecloth and stood up, looking at Corcoran, her hands on her hips.

"Do I look like I have time to baby-sit all the out of work salmon fishermen on the whole damn coast? He's probably sick of hauling crab, Gabe. He's a salmon guy, and the Chinook ban is killing him. He's probably sleeping off a bender somewhere." Abby ran her hand over the already flat tablecloth, once again not looking at the deputy.

Corcoran shifted his feet, and adjusted his belt again. "You call me if you hear anything, Ok?" he said, and turned to face me and the door. Ignoring me, he walked to the door. This time, I caught the door before it could begin to close, and followed him out to his car.

"She didn't see him there last night," I said before he could reach for the door handle.

"What's that?" he asked, finally acknowledging my presence.

"She asked the singer last night about someone named Gill. Like she was surprised that he wasn't there. Like the singer should have known where he was. Is Gill a common name around here?" I asked, moving around to put myself between the deputy and the car.

He looked at me again, his face looking like he had just swallowed spoiled milk. "Redheaded girl, plays that flute?"

"Pennywhistle, actually. Name of the band. She hadn't seen him either, seemed annoyed at the question."

Corcoran reached for the door handle and opened the car door. He began wedging himself into the car while looking up at me. "When you make your reports to that Porter woman, you copy me on it, you hear? And I get my copy first." He pulled the seat belt over and struggled to get it fastened.

"That shouldn't be a problem," I said. "Like I said, I'm here to help."

Corcoran snorted, and slammed the car door shut. I moved away from the car, and he backed out of the lot, turned, and carefully made his way to the highway.

Footsteps behind me made me turn around. Randy Hanson, a large camera bag in his hand, watched Corcoran drive off. "Getting any help on the story?" he asked, turning to me.

"Well, like I said, I usually just do travel pieces. This kind of stuff is really out of my league. Interesting though. Do you know where Pelican Point is?"

"Yeah, about three miles up. Nice walk if you're not carrying a ten pound lens," he said, holding up his camera bag. "I'm going up to Fort Bragg, I could drop you off, and you could walk back."

"You think Fort Bragg has a rental car place? I should probably get my own wheels if this vacation is turning into work."

"We can check it out. Be nice to have company on the trip." Hanson smiled, and I smiled back. He walked over to a large extended cab pickup truck, and motioned for me to get in.

"What's at Pelican Point for you?" he asked as we drove north.

"I wanted to take some pictures of tire tracks," I said. "Assuming that Gill Barnett's car was parked off the pavement." I explained about the deputy's missing person case.

"Sounds like fun," Hanson said. "We'll pull off a little ways down the road and hike back, so we don't disturb anything."

Pelican Point had a large dirt parking area, still damp from the recent rains. Gill Barnett's car was still there. As we approached the dirt area on foot, walking along the side of the highway, I brought out my pocket camera.

There was a jumble of tire tracks leading from the highway onto the parking area. I took a picture, but nothing there was going to be of much help. Walking carefully on the high spots to avoid the mud, we approached the car. I took some more photos of the car and the ground around it.

There were three distinct tread marks near the car. One set was from Barnett's car, clearly leading up to the rear tires. Another fresh set were probably Corcoran's car. Footprints leading from that set to Barnett's car were small and deep, which I took to indicate the heavy-set deputy. The tire tracks and footsteps went over the earlier tracks from Barnett's car. The third set of tracks went over Barnett's tracks, but under Corcoran's.

"So, Barnett parked here, and then another car parked next to him. Then Corcoran came along and parked where the second car had been, so that car must have left sometime earlier," I said to Hanson. He had brought out his own camera, replaced the long lens with a smaller one, and was taking pictures of everything I was.

The area between the two cars was trampled with Corcoran's footprints, and was pretty much useless as evidence. I walked carefully around to the other side of the car, stepping on rocks, grass, and firm ground where I could, so as not to leave my own footprints. Hanson did the same, carefully stepping only where I stepped.

It was tedious, and much of the ground on that side of the car was firm and graveled, not conducive to leaving clean footprints. But about fifteen feet from the car, a short set of prints led towards the guardrail. These were larger prints, with a waffle pattern, like work boots. They disappeared in the gravel, and I followed in the direction they led. Close to the guardrail, there were clear prints again, the same waffle pattern, now standing, feet together. Next to them were the prints of smaller women's shoes, pointed toe, deep heel marks, also standing next to the waffle prints. Beyond the guardrail, the cliff dropped off vertically to the rough surf below, perhaps a hundred feet or more. The view was fantastic. I took a few shots of the cliff and the water below, and the ground around us.

Hanson was aiming his camera at the ground towards the car, playing with the zoom lens. I looked over to where he was aiming the camera, and then carefully made my way across, keeping to the gravel and the occasional rock. There was the woman's footprint again, leading back to the car. I took some more photos. The ground was muddy and soft for a good ten feet around the footprint, and I could make out waffled prints leading away from the car, and women's prints leading both away from the car and back to the car.

Hanson and I both searched carefully, but could find nothing more. No waffle prints led back to the car, only towards the cliff.

The ride up to Fort Bragg took a while, and Hanson and I considered as many possibilities as we could find.

"So, he gets drunk, starts to drive home, decides it isn't safe, and calls someone to pick him up," I began.

"Usually, that would be the wife," Hanson said.

"But since she's the one reporting him missing, that would seem unlikely. Unless she was covering up having pushed him off the cliff instead of taking him home," I joked.

"No sign of a struggle," Hanson corrected.

"And no waffle prints leading back to the car," I pointed out, "but the ground wasn't all that good for footprints, and Corcoran had messed up the area around the car pretty thoroughly."

"So he calls a friend, a woman, to pick him up, and while he waits, he takes a leak over the cliff. She comes along and carries his drunk ass back to the car," Hanson said, taking a turn in the road a little too sharply.

"Her returning steps would have been much deeper than her outward steps," I said.

"He walks along the guardrail for a while, and she walks straight back to the car and picks him up at the highway." Hanson made another sharp turn, and I considered letting him concentrate on his driving.

"So he's passed out at some woman friend's house, he's without a car, and he's afraid to call home," I said, disregarding my safety. "It's probably something that lame and ordinary. Most things are."

In Fort Bragg, Hanson dropped me off at an Enterprise car rental, and went off to do his errands. I rented a Camry and drove back to Pelican Point.

Carefully following the tracks of the woman's car, I looked for any evidence that it had stopped anywhere but next to Barnett's car, and for any sign of Barnett's waffled feet near the tracks. But the tread marks were even all along the way from the highway to the parked car, with no sign of starting and stopping, and no footprints anywhere except where Corcoran had trampled all the evidence into the mud.

I walked carefully along the guardrail, leaving no prints myself, but looking at every small stone that might have been pressed into the mud by a large man, and looked for any grass or weeds that might have been damaged recently. It was slow work, and completely unrewarding.

I went back to the pair of footprints by the guardrail. I sat on the rail, and tried to picture the scene the night before. I had arrived at McDougal's a little before eight o'clock. The band was already playing, and Gill Barnett was expected to be there. His wife had told the deputy that he was usually home by eleven.

There were three women I knew of who Gill Barnett might have called to pick him up. One was his wife. The other two were Abigail McDougal and the singer.

I didn't have much in the way of equipment with me. I had no measuring tape or ruler. But I did have the car rental receipt in my shirt pocket. I unfolded it, and placed it next to the footprints and took another picture. I could bring the picture up on the laptop computer and get an accurate measurement that way.

Gill Barnett was Lee Aleada's least forthcoming interview. Now he was missing. I had a tire print and a footprint of a woman who may have been involved somehow. I looked at the footprints again. That did not look like the footprint of a fisherman's wife to me.

I drove back to McDougal's, and parked at the far end of the parking lot. This allowed me to casually snap photos of car tires as I walked back to the lodge. I kept the camera in my hand as if I were merely carrying it, letting it swing with my stride. The photos would look tilted and wild, but the tires would be in focus.

I put the camera back in my pocket as I entered the lodge. As usual, there was no one in reception. I peeked into the dining room where we had eaten breakfast, and it was also empty. I finally pulled open the big door to the bar, and found George Franco sitting alone at one of the tables, eating a sandwich. Abigail McDougal was behind the bar, wiping something down. I don't think I'd ever seen her when she wasn't busy doing something related to the resort.

There was a short list of sandwiches on a chalkboard behind her. I sat down at the bar, nodded to Abigail, and studied the list. I had four choices. Noticing the sandwich grill near my stool, I picked the one that would keep Abigail close to me for a while.

"How's the grilled Reuben today?" I asked.

"Same as yesterday," Abby said, wiping her hands on a towel.

"Good enough for me," I said. "I'd like the Reuben then, and a Diet Coke."

"The Reuben isn't diet food, you know," she said, reaching for the rye bread.

"I like Diet Coke better than the sugar kind. Seems to hit my thirst better," I said. "That was a pretty good band last night. They play here much?"

"Pretty much every night. They're cheap, and local."

I watched as she made the sandwich. "I left early last night. My headache and all. How late do they usually play?"

She pointed to a sign behind her. "Bar closes at eleven. Band is done at ten thirty. You want to party all night you go into town. I have to be up early for breakfast, and there's just me and Maria right now, until I get someone to take McDougal's place."

I looked at her as she buttered the top of the sandwich. She did not look up at me. "You call your father 'McDougal'?" I asked.

Now she looked up at me. "People called him Danny, or McDougal. I could never call him Danny. Be damned if I'd call the old fart 'Daddy'." She went back to the sandwich, placing it on the grill. The butter sizzled.

"So," I said, keeping a jovial tone, "what part of things did McDougal run around here? What kind of help are you looking for? I might know someone."

She studied the sandwich, seeming to consider whether to bother answering me. Then she spoke. "He did breakfast, for one, so I could sleep in. He fixed what broke. He was chatty. People liked that. I'm not. And he said he handled the books, the turkey."

She turned the sandwich, and the butter sizzled again.

"Your bookkeeping? For the lodge?" I asked.

"Total mess. I tried to make sense of what was there, but even the damn checkbook wasn't balanced. He had piles of receipts in a box, checks from guests that hadn't been cashed that were weeks old, bills he hadn't paid. Nothing written down. How the hell am I supposed to do the taxes? There's a quarterly estimated tax due in December, and I couldn't find any hint of what he paid in the last three quarters."

I tried not to sound eager, but my heart rate had increased as I thought about getting access to the lodge's records. "I could definitely help there," I said. "I have an accountant friend in the city who owes me a big favor, and she'd absolutely love it here. If you comp her a room, she could clean up the bookkeeping in a couple of days, easily."

She slid the spatula under the sandwich and slipped it onto a plate decorated with parsley and a sliced pickle. She looked me in the eye as she handed me the plate. "I'll keep that in mind."

She filled a glass with Diet Coke from the fountain and placed it in front of me. I looked over the bar, but could not see her feet. She was a tall woman, however, and the feet at Pelican Point had been small.

I finished the sandwich in less time than it had taken to make. Abigail McDougal cleaned the grill and finally left the bar area and I watched as she went through the big door to the reception area. She was wearing running shoes.

I went back to my room, and got out the laptop computer. I loaded the photos into it, and brought up a photo editor to crop the images of the tire tracks and the tires in the parking lot. None of the tires in the lot looked like a match to the tracks, but I am no expert. I pulled up the email window and attached the photos to a new message. I entered what I had overheard in the bar, what I had found at Pelican Point, my discussion with the deputy, and my guess at Abigail's shoe size.

I took a minute to look up the deputy's office email address, sent the mail to Gabriel Corcoran, copied Silvia Porter, and sent the mail.

I started another mail, this time only to Silvia. I asked for Valerie Wilson, her forensic accountant, and explained my conversation with Abigail McDougal. I also went into more detail on my discussions with the other guests, and speculation about Gill Barnett.

After I had sent that mail, I did a search for the band Pennywhistle, adding some local town names to constrain the search. The band had a MySpace page, and photos.

The singer's name was Penelope Dixon. Most of the photos were amateurish, blurred from movement in dim lighting, but it was clearly the same woman. The page was difficult to read, dark fonts on dark backgrounds, but once I selected all the text and copied into a word processor, I had nice black letters on white, and I could adjust the font size to something my old eyes could read without headache.

There were short bio pieces on each of the band members, lyrics to the songs, blog entries about venues and events, and other trivia. I concentrated on the parts that related to Penelope Dixon. She needed an editor pretty badly.

Most of the stuff was useless. However, one piece referred to her "private" MySpace page, and hinted at the treasures there.

So I did another search. I limited it to MySpace pages, and threw in names of local towns, some of the band venues, first names of band members, and the names of some of the songs. I whittled and played with the search for about twenty minutes, but I finally found the page.

She used a pseudonym, TinyDancer1221, but it was definitely Penelope Dixon. The same spelling errors and choice of words, and mentions of singing in various locales in the area. It was a diary, sparsely done, sometimes weekly, sometimes twice in a day, with occasional long gaps.

A Quiet Place to Die

There was too much there to read all at once, so I selected the text and copied it into my phone to read later.

I walked back down to the reception desk, and again no one was there. I could hear some machinery running somewhere outside, so I walked around the building until I could recognize the sound of laundry machines. The door to the laundry room was open, and I went inside. A woman was loading sheets into a big commercial washer.

"Hello," I said. "I wonder if you could help me."

The woman turned around to face me. She was perhaps 30, with long black hair and dark eyes. She smiled and said "Yes?"

"I was wondering if there was a place nearby where I could buy a teddy bear for my niece. For her birthday?" I asked.

She looked at me as if she hadn't understood. "A teddy bear?" she asked, with a slight accent, rocking an imaginary baby in her arms.

"Yes, for my niece, for her birthday," I repeated.

"Not around here," she said. "Maybe in Mendocino they have those, but not around here."

"Well then," I said cheerily. "I guess I'm off to Mendocino. Thank you very much!"

She grinned and waved as I turned to go. I waved back, and walked back out to my car. Mendocino was back north, on the way to Fort Bragg.

On the way up the highway, as I passed Pelican Point, I saw a tow truck getting ready to take Gill Barnett's car somewhere. I was glad we had stopped earlier, before more of the evidence was obliterated. I slowed a bit, trying to make out if the driver was alone, but I could not even make out the driver. I passed by, and continued up the winding coast road.

I slowed again whenever I came to a little knot of civilization. They were few and far between, and usually tiny, but I looked for tourist shops or toys stores where Danny McDougal might have purchased the teddy bear, but had no luck. Out of habit, I photographed each side of the road at these spots, reaching my hand out the window to shoot the right side from over the roof. If I had a question later, I could always study the photos on the laptop.

Mendocino is a small place, and probably has less than a thousand permanent residents. I drove completely through it the first time, and doubled back when I realized I had run out of town. I wound through most of the main streets in the car, stopping occasionally to snap photos. Finally, I parked, and went back over promising areas on foot.

There were several little tourist shops that looked like they might have teddy bears. The second one I tried pointed me to a small toy store down the street. The store had a couple of tourists in it looking around, and the cashier perked up as I entered.

I took out my phone and brought up a picture of the teddy bear that had been found in McDougal's car.

"Do you carry teddy bears like this?" I said, holding up the tiny picture to the cashier. He studied it for a bit, and I couldn't blame him for not seeing much detail.

"We have a few over here," he said, walking to a corner of the store. There were three different types, and I zoomed in on the picture in the phone to see if I could match details.

"I'm trying to get one for my niece that matches one her friend has," I said. "They said they got it here. I wonder, is there a way you could check to see which kind you sold to Danny McDougal? It would be some time in September."

The man looked doubtful. He walked over to a door that was halfway open and shouted into a small hallway. "Mom? Can you help this guy? He needs you to look up something on the computer."

An older woman eventually came out of the door, polishing her glasses on her shirttail.

"How can I help you?" she said, when the man waved her in my direction. I explained my story again.

The woman went to the cash register, which was a computer screen and a keyboard, and hunted through screens of menus before she found what she was looking for. I spelled McDougal's name, and I was greatly surprised at my luck when she found a receipt for a teddy bear, dated September 27th.

"Excellent!," I said, not having to fake my elation. "He had it gift wrapped," I said. "Who would have done the wrapping, do you know?"

"That would be me," the woman said.

"Oh, great!" I said. "Do you think you could wrap one for me the same way? The girls are close friends, and they love to do everything together the same way."

"I remember that man. Kind of tall, thick gray hair, mustache?" she said.

"That's Danny," I said.

"I remember him, because we had quite a chat. I asked him if it was for his granddaughter and he laughed at me, because he had a four-year-old daughter. He asked me to fill out the birthday card because his hands were too shaky to write it up as nice as he wanted. Such a nice man, such a big smile."

I smiled as big as I could. "What did he have you write on the card?" I asked.

"Oh, it was something simple. Happy Birthday Susan or something like that. But that wasn't the name, something out of the bible I think. Sarah. Yes, Happy Birthday Sarah."

"Not Abigail?" I asked.

"Is that your niece's friend's name?" she asked.

"No, I was just making a joke. Abigail is his secretary," I explained.

"No, it was definitely Sarah. I remember asking if it had an 'H' at the end."

I bought the teddy bear, and had it gift-wrapped. Silvia was paying for it; I might just send it to her.

I got back to the lodge before dark. The parking lot was filling up with bar patrons, and the band had not yet arrived. I walked around, shooting pictures of the lodge that included tire treads. I watched each car, hoping to see Penelope Dixon step out of one. I waited a long time. I saw one or two people I was sure were members of the band, but no Ms. Dixon.

I was about to give up when a Miata drove up with the top down, and a orange flame of long hair waved from the driver's seat. Penelope Dixon unfastened her seat belt and stood up on the seat, then jumped over the door to land on the ground. Either the door handle was broken, or she liked making an entrance with her skirt flying up to her waist.

I waited until she had entered the lodge, then I took a picture of the Miata's tire tread. The flash on the camera lit up the front of the lodge. It was getting dark.

I walked into the lodge, and followed a couple into the bar. The band was setting up, and the crowd was still light. I went to the bar and caught Abigail's attention.

"Diet Coke?" I asked. The noise level in the room was already starting to rise.

"I can see I'm going to make a lot of money off of *you* tonight," she said, filling a glass from the fountain. I took out a five-dollar bill and made sure she saw me put it into the tip jar, and handed her another one for the drink. I didn't wait for the change, but went to find a spot at the edge of the stage where I expected Rafael Gonzales and Johnny McCarthy to show up. I was not expecting Gill Barnett.

Nursing my Coke, I watched the band set up, and watched people in the bar settle into their places. I turned the flash off on the camera, and rested it on the table as I took candid shots of people, the table acting as a tripod to steady the camera in the dim light.

Randy Hanson came in, and I waved him over to my table. He nodded and pointed to the bar, where he went to place an order. A minute later, he was setting his beer down at my table and pulling up a chair.

"The singer's name is Penelope Dixon," I said. "She drives a Mazda Miata. It's parked out front, next to the footbridge and the koi pond. I got some shots of the tires."

Hanson nodded. "Everyone around here calls her Penny," he said, and pointed to the woman, who had just come onto the stage.

I looked at her feet. Small pointed toed shoes with a raised heel. They looked like they would match the footprints at Pelican Point. I was pretty sure the tire tread would match the tracks there as well.

"Did you know Gill Barnett?" I asked, raising my voice over the crowd noise. At least the band had not begun to play.

Hanson nodded his head and took another swallow from his beer.

"I'm sitting up here so I can meet some of the locals, maybe make some friends, see what people know," I explained.

"Jennifer Strike usually shows up. She has a thing for the bass player. But she's a photographer, so she and I have gotten to know each other, compare equipment and stuff. She can introduce you to some people. If I see her, I'll call her over."

I nodded vigorously, as the band was tuning up, and I didn't want to lose my voice too early in the evening.

The band launched into their first number, and all hope of conversation evaporated. Penny Dixon played the pennywhistle into the microphone, and stomped her feet in time to the music when it was someone else's turn for a solo. I turned the flash back on and took some shots of the band, making sure I got some good views of her feet when she raised them.

As they started on the second song, Randy Hanson started waving at someone entering the bar. I turned and saw a slightly overweight young woman in a shapeless flannel shirt and baggy jeans coming over to our table.

Randy shouted to her as she was taking a seat. "Jimmy Davis," he said, pointing at me. "Newspaper reporter." He pointed to the woman. "Jennifer Strike."

I nodded at her, and extended my hand. She grinned at my nod and looked at the speakers as she shook my hand. Randy pointed to his beer and stood up, pantomiming an offer to get her one. She nodded, and he left for the bar.

I held the camera up as if to take a picture of her, and pantomimed asking permission. She laughed and shrugged, and I framed the shot so the bass player was in the background. I handed her the camera to show her the shot. She looked at the screen and laughed, then started to smooth her hair.

Hanson returned with two beers and placed one in front of Jennifer. He tried to say something, but she shook her head and pointed to the speakers. I got out my phone. Pulling out the sliding keyboard, I texted "Hi there!" and showed her the screen. She laughed again, and waved hello.

I texted again. "do u no gill barnett?"

She nodded vigorously, and took the phone, texting "he is missing."

I took the phone back. "ne idea where he mite be?" I texted, and handed the phone to her.

She shook her head. "rafe mite". She pointed to a large man two tables down. She stood up, fished her own phone from her front pocket, and opened it. She typed something, and walked over to Rafael Gonzales' table and showed him the screen. He looked up at her, and she pointed in our direction.

Gonzales and another man got up from their table and accompanied Jennifer over to ours. All of us looked at one another for a few seconds, each aware the speaking wasn't going to work. Gonzales aimed a thumb at the door, and Hanson and I stood up. Together, the five of us left the bar.

When the big door swung shut behind us, my ears were ringing, and everything sounded muffled and dead. We walked past the reception desk and out into the parking lot.

"Jimmy Davis," I said, and extended a hand to Gonzales. He took my hand reluctantly, and said "Rafe. This is Johnny Mac." He indicated the other man.

"I write for local newspapers. I was talking with Gabe Corcoran, the sheriff's deputy, this morning and I offered to help find Gill Barnett. Has he talked with you guys yet?"

"Yeah. He's useless," Johnny Mac said. "We didn't go out today. Spent the day looking for Gill. Checked all the places we could think of, drove all over. Nobody's seen him. We came back here in case he shows up. He likes the band a lot. Weird him not being here."

"He wasn't here yesterday, either, was he?" I asked.

"He was here for a little while," Gonzales said. "Then he was gone. They found his car over at Pelican Point."

"We went out there," Hanson said. "Corcoran had trampled all over the place, messed up footprints and tire tracks, everything."

"Can you think of any reason he would leave town without telling anyone? His wife, his shipmates, his drinking buddies?" I asked.

Gonzales shook his head. "He loves his kids. Takes them to school every day, best part of the day for him, unless we're catching salmon."

"He and his wife get along?" I asked.

Gonzales looked at me, then at Johnny Mac. "You write newspaper stories?" he asked.

"This isn't for a story. I don't do those kinds of stories anyway. I'm just trying to help Corcoran find a missing person," I said. I didn't mention that Corcoran would probably rather that I didn't help.

"We found women's footprints at Pelican Point," Hanson said.

"We think they are associated with tire tracks that were left after Barnett's car was parked, but before Corcoran's car got there. There's no telling the actual timing, though. It could be that some woman came along and saw the car there, stopped to check it out, and reported it to the sheriff's office." I didn't want everyone to jump to the conclusions I had. I had no justification for mine.

"You think maybe Cathy drove up there?" Gonzales asked.

"Cathy is his wife?" Hanson asked.

"They only have the one car," Johnny Mac pointed out. "That's why he has to take the kids to school."

"She could have had someone take her there," Gonzales said.

"There was only one set of women's footprints, and one set of men's. Except for Corcoran's." It was good to get them talking. They were accepting my role. We were on the same side, and I was no longer a stranger.

"It could have been anybody," Jennifer said. "Some woman saw the car and stopped, like Jimmy said."

"He's got to be in trouble somewhere. He wouldn't leave his kids if he could help it. Maybe he fell off the cliff," Johnny Mac said.

"No sign of that," I said. "The footprints ended at the guardrail. There was no sign of any struggle, no sign of any falling rocks or a landslide. If he went into the water, he dove in. Or jumped from the guardrail."

"Or was pushed," Gonzales said. "By someone he knew and didn't expect would push him."

"Did he have any enemies?" I asked. The group got quiet. I could have taken that either as a yes or as a no, but Johnny Mac shook his head.

"Everybody liked Gill," he said. Gonzales nodded.

"If he was a victim of foul play," I said, "that would be the second murder in a month, maybe the third. Could any of the three deaths be connected?"

"That Lee guy was looking into Danny's accident. If that wasn't an accident, he could have been getting too close," Jennifer said. "That's what everyone around here has been talking about."

"But Gill didn't know anything about that," Johnny Mac said. "We kept saying to the deputy and that Lee guy, Gill just goes off alone sometimes. He had nothing against Danny – nobody did, except maybe Abby."

"But Gill got all upset about all the questions they were asking. Real mad. Said it was nobody's business where he was that night. He put that big dent in his car with his foot he was so mad," Jennifer said.

Gonzales didn't like how that sounded. "He just gets upset sometimes. What we should be looking at is where he might have gone, or who might have taken him somewhere."

"Or who might have pushed him off of Pelican Point," Johnny Mac said.

"Suppose," said Hanson, "he knew who shot the insurance guy. That guy might have needed to shut him up."

"He would have told Corcoran," Gonzales said.

The group was silent for a few seconds.

"If he knew, what would keep him from telling Corcoran?" Jennifer asked. "Maybe he was protecting someone."

"Maybe he found out recently," Johnny Mac said. "Maybe he was going to tell Corcoran."

I put up my hand to end the speculation. "I'll be here every evening at this time, so I can keep everyone up to date on what Corcoran and I find out," I said, knowing full well that the deputy was not likely to share much with me.

I fished out some business cards from my wallet. "You can contact me on my cell, or by email, or by finding me here in person. You're his best friends – you'll probably know things before I do. But anything I find out I'll share with you as soon as I get it."

They took the cards. Gonzales held his up to the light from the lodge to read it. All it says is freelance journalist, and the contact info.

"So, there are a few things we can do right away. First, if we can establish a timeline and find out when Gill was last seen, that should help. Also, the time when he was first noticed missing might also be important."

"We hauled in at about four thirty," Gonzales offered. "We scrubbed down the boat, and took it back to the slip at about what? Sixish?" he said, looking at Johnny Mac.

"More like six thirty. We showered at the marina and changed out of work clothes. Gill was the first to leave. He drove off while Rafe and I were still getting dressed," Johnny Mac said.

A Quiet Place to Die

"We usually meet here after work for a beer. Gill never showed up," Gonzales said.

"So, just before seven then?" I said. They nodded. "And when did you first find out he hadn't come home?"

"Catherine called my house at about two in the morning," Gonzales said. "She called again at about five."

I checked the notes in my cell phone. "I don't have the time the sheriff was notified. Do you know when he was called?" I didn't want to mention that the deputy had not informed me.

"I told Catherine to call him after the second call. So maybe she called a little after five in the morning."

I added this to my notes.

"If you think of anything else I should know, get it to me as soon as you can. In the meantime, I think my editor is going to pay for the next round of beers." I waved towards the lodge, and we walked back into the bar together.

Abigail McDougal watched as the two fishermen reclaimed their table, and Jennifer and Hanson sat down with them. She put down her towel as I approached the bar.

"Two pitchers of whatever Rafe and Johnny Mac were drinking," I said.

"You're making friends fast," she said, apparently not really caring.

"It's easy when you're buying," I said. "Nice people, though. Everyone around here seems nice. Is it something in the water?"

"Maybe. I don't drink water," she said, putting one pitcher on the bar and starting to fill the other.

"Well then," I said, ignoring her innuendo. "In that case, let me buy you a beer sometime when it slows down enough for you to get a minute."

"Fresh out of minutes," she said, putting the second pitcher up on the bar. I put down a bill and took the pitchers, not waiting for change.

I brought the two pitchers over to the table, dodging a couple trying to dance to the fast music. I set them down on the table, and went back for glasses. Abby had five beer glasses lined up on the bar, and I took them in my arms wordlessly, and made my way back to the table. Mercifully, the band had just finished, and I could get a word in.

"Is Abby always so friendly?" I asked.

"She's got issues," Jennifer said. "Don't take it personally."

"Is she still working it out after her father's death?" I asked.

Gonzales laughed. "Not hardly. She's always been that way. She and Danny fought like cats, all the time. They hated each other, long as I've known the two of them. I think she's relieved he finally kicked off."

Johnny Mac rushed to her defense. "He was a jerk, but he was her father. She just doesn't show her emotions, ever. It's a defense mechanism, living with him all those years."

I was about to follow up, but the band started playing again. I watched the singer dance around and spin. It seemed like she was not playing to the front row as much as she had when I first arrived. She was not making eye contact with Rafe or Johnny Mac. It might have been the presence of three outsiders at the table with the two fishermen. Maybe I was just seeing things that weren't there.

After an hour or so, the pitchers were empty, and even Jennifer had given up trying to talk. Rafe and Johnny Mac were not as jovial and carefree as they had been the first night, and they seemed self-conscious, as if enjoying themselves when their friend was missing was not going to happen.

A Quiet Place to Die

I stood up to leave, and the rest of the group took the cue without words. We walked out of the bar, and the now familiar hush fell over the world as my ears adjusted to the relative quiet of the parking lot.

"See you tomorrow," I said as Rafe and Johnny Mac walked to their cars. Randy walked towards his room, and Jennifer walked over to the band's van, probably to wait for the bass player. I went up to my room.

It was still early, and I sat down at the laptop, which was still showing the web page of TinyDancer1221.

I started reading. Penelope Dixon was something of a drama queen. Every small detail of her life was suffused with often-tragic emotional detail. However, little details, like references to divorced parents, or suicidal friends, or episodes of bulimia, seemed genuine, if overstated.

One item caught my eye. She referred to an affair with a married man. I skimmed quickly to find details that might identify the person. He had broken it off recently, perhaps as recently as last week.

I read a few previous entries. She referred to him as Starfish in the web page. Long paragraphs about how wonderful he made her feel, about cutting the music short so she could have more time for secret meetings with him. He was strong, and tasted like beer.

I made a list of the times when the two had been together. It seemed to be mostly after the band had quit for the evening, or an occasional weekend afternoon.

If Penelope Dixon had been having an affair with Gill Barnett, and it had ended badly as late as last week, would he have called her when he needed a ride home, leaving his car at Pelican Point? Did Gill even have a cell phone with which to make such a call? I would have to ask Rafe or Johnny Mac tomorrow.

I read about TinyDancer1221 until it got late. I was getting to know quite a bit about Penelope Dixon, and was becoming somewhat fond of her, in a fatherly way. How much was fiction and how much hyperbole I could not tell, but I would have to be careful not to let on I knew so much, should I get the chance to speak to her.

One item explained the name, though. On December 21, someone had wished her a happy birthday. That is where the 12 and the 21 in the name came from. All of the comments were anonymous. It would be nice to know which of her friends were privy to the details she provided in this public diary, and if any of them might know who Starfish was.

Before turning in, I checked my email. It was a good thing I did – Valerie Wilson was coming over in the morning. She was aware there was a chance she'd be going right back, but I was counting on being able to charm the ice from Abigail McDougal and get Valerie a look at the lodge's books. I'm vain that way. Sometimes I get lucky.

Which is bullshit, I said to myself. I needed help. And I didn't want Abby to say no, so I didn't ask. I was no good at this stuff anymore. Whatever it was that I had that made me good at my job had been taken away by that bullet. I touched my shoulder, feeling for the places that had once been smooth. What was I trying to prove?

§

Valerie Wilson

The blue jay was at my window again in the morning. He was insistent. I got up, showered, and was dressed before seven.

The early morning air was chill and I was not dressed for it. Dew had collected on all horizontal surfaces in what seemed like the entire county, and everything I touched was cold and wet. I made my way into the dining room, wondering how early I had to get up to beat George and Gina to breakfast.

Apparently, earlier than I had. George had his back to me, but Gina waved as soon as I entered. She was dressed in several layers that concealed whatever figure might be underneath.

I held my hand in a high-five to George, hoping to avoid crushed knuckles. He returned the gesture, and I sat down.

"How's the real estate writing going?" he asked. I pulled my chair under the heavy table. It seemed to be a theme of the place — everything was made of huge thick planks of wood.

"I'm afraid it's going to have to wait," I said. "I'm helping the sheriff's department with a missing person case. A local fisherman, a regular at the bar, left his car by the side of the road a mile or so north of here."

"I saw you talking to the cops," Gina said. That did not surprise me. I made a note to take advantage of the observation skills of a gifted gossip.

"So how did you get deputized?" George asked.

"He probably thinks I have investigative journalism skills or something," I said. "But really, I just offered my help. You never know what might make a good story, or when you might be working on one thing and stumble into something else you can sell to an editor. That's how the freelance thing works." Or at least how it should work. My bullshit was falling over itself.

"Is there much money in that?" he asked.

"If there is, I have yet to find it. It keeps me in beer and peanuts, though. And I get to write off expenses, like the lodge bill here." I could hear some banging of pans and cupboard doors behind the door leading to the kitchen.

"I write everything off," George said. "I own the business, and just about everything is a business expense. It doesn't make stuff free, though, just cheaper. Too bad about that, eh?" He laughed at his wit.

Abigail came out with coffee. "Good morning, Abby," I said. "Do you ever use the cappuccino machine in the bar for coffee in the morning?"

"Bar's not open in the morning," she said. "You want whiskey in that?"

"No, no, it will be just fine, thanks. I was just curious," I said, accepting the cup and saucer and its sad contents. I took a sip to confirm my suspicions, and added milk and sugar. The things we do for our drug fix in the morning.

Randy Hanson came in at about the time I had finished the cup. He pulled up a chair next to Gina, across from me.

"Anything new?" he asked.

"Maybe," I said. "Last night, when we were in front of the stage, did the singer seem less interested in entertaining Rafe and Johnny than the day before?"

Hanson considered for a moment. "Come to think of it, you might be right. But she's been off and on with those guys for a while, mostly off the last week or so. Of course, Gill is usually with them, and the three of them get a lot rowdier than just the two. Is it relevant?"

"It might be. I'll let you know if something comes of it. I'm trying to get a feel for the relationships around here, who knows who, that kind of thing."

"You should ask Maria," Gina offered. "Maids know everything. A lot of people think she can't understand English, so they say things in front of her they wouldn't usually say."

"I got to meet the young lady yesterday," I said. "Charming woman, very helpful."

"Really?" Gina asked.

"Definitely charming," Hanson confirmed. "But I find her much more interesting when I speak Spanish with her. She's quite a bright young woman; she's just a little hesitant with her English. I'm trying to talk her into taking classes, to get her confidence up."

"My, I never would have thought," Gina said. "You speak Spanish?"

"A little," Hanson said. "I like to stay in practice, use it when I can. She speaks better English than I speak Spanish, but she corrects me, which is great. Most people just ignore my awful Spanish and try to keep the conversation short."

More coffee arrived. I noticed Hanson was also diluting his with milk and sugar. He seemed to stir it much longer than necessary, as if lost in thought. I broke the silence.

"I hear Rafe Gonzalez and Danny McDougal had a dustup the night he died," I said. "Were you there? Did you see what happened?"

Hanson looked up from his coffee stirring. "Yeah, I was there. Not much of a fight."

"Do you know what it was about?" I asked, reaching for more milk, and doing my own thoughtful stirring.

"You can't hear shit in that place when the band is going. But those two had been at each other for a couple of days." He lowered his voice and leaned over to me. "Something about Abby, I think."

Gina looked at the two of us. "About..." she said, nodding her head towards the kitchen door.

Hanson nodded. "They were both really loaded. Tanked. The old man can hold it though. He's had years and years of steady practice. They were shouting about something. Rafe took a swing at him, but didn't connect. Then the old guy hit him in the face, while he still had the long neck in his fist. I couldn't tell if the bottle hit Rafe in the face or the fist with the bottle neck in it did, but he went down hard."

Gina was fascinated. She leaned over the big table, her chin almost meeting the tablecloth. "What happened then?"

"Danny just went over to the bar, picked up a whiskey bottle and a box of something out of the freezer, and left. Gill and Johnny Mac picked up Rafe, and the band kept playing. That was it."

Gina seemed disappointed. She sat back in her chair and put her hands in her lap.

"Do you remember what time it was?" I asked.

"Not late," Hanson said. He looked into his empty coffee cup for inspiration. "The band quit early. Gill and Penny went off somewhere, and Rafe and Johnny Mac went out back and Rafe puked his guts out into the blackberry thicket."

This didn't seem right to me. I pulled out my phone, and waited while it woke up. The notes from Lee Aleada took a while to scan through, but I found his record of the interview with Johnny Mac.

"Johnny Mac said that he and Rafe were out night fishing when Danny McDougal died," I said. Gina, George, and Hanson were all looking at me as if I were reading out winning lottery ticket numbers. "Did Rafe look like he was in shape for going out on the water?"

Hanson considered this. "It wouldn't be my first guess. I would think Johnny Mac probably drove him home to sleep it off."

I pushed back in my chair. "So neither Johnny Mac nor Rafe have an alibi for the night Danny died. They made up a story about night fishing to tell Corcoran and Lee Aleada. Why would they do that?" The last comment was rhetorical, but that seemed lost on Gina.

"But he died of a heart attack, didn't he?" she said, her head cocked like a cocker spaniel wondering when you were going to throw a ball.

"He died of suffocation," I said. "As if someone had found him passed out in his car, and had put a plastic bag over his head for a while until he stopped breathing. No signs of a struggle, no strangulation marks, no cloth fibers in his nose or mouth, but hemorrhaging consistent with strangulation. And a very high alcohol level in his blood, indicating that he was likely unconscious and unable to resist."

Gina sat back, her eyes wide. "Oh, my," she said. "Everyone just talked about his 'accident'. Nobody said he was murdered. Two people murdered just as we started our vacation! This used to be such a nice quiet place!"

Hanson looked in my direction, pushing his hat up higher on his head. "So you think maybe Rafe and Johnny Mac were driving home, and saw his car pulled over, and decided to finish the fight with a plastic bag?"

I smiled. "Doesn't seem that likely, does it? Not much of a motive for Johnny Mac, is there? But what if Rafe had tried to drive himself home?"

"And he'd still be drunk," George said, "so he might have acted on impulse. Or maybe it wasn't about the fight, but about what led to the fight. Like maybe he was trying to kill him in the bar when he took the first swing."

Hanson pointed his finger at me. "That would make Rafe Gonzales the top suspect in the shooting, too. If Aleada was getting close to finding out, Rafe might think he needed to get rid of him."

I looked over at Gina. "This is all pure speculation, remember. There is no proof of any of this. If word got out that we were spreading rumors about Rafe Gonzales being a killer, he might get very angry with whoever was spreading those rumors. So don't tell anyone, they might get into trouble by spreading it around."

That last bit was to mollify Gina, whose face was getting upset as she realized I was calling her a gossip. She took the face saving gesture, and nodded vigorously. I figured the news would reach Timbuktu by nightfall. That was good for me. The more people talked, the more I would find out.

I pressed on. "After all, McDougal's death could have been a suicide. Suppose he was depressed, and the alcohol wasn't helping. So he pulls over to the side of the road, puts a bag over his head, and suffocates himself. Then Abigail drives around looking for him, finds him, and removes the bag so it will look like a heart attack, so she gets the insurance money. That scenario is why Lee Aleada was out here investigating anyway. He was an insurance investigator."

George leaned in. "So when he starts to figure it out, she takes the old man's gun out of the box in the bar and shoots Aleada. So she gets the money."

Gina shushed him quickly, pointing to the door to the kitchen.

"So," I said. "You see, two entirely different scenarios, each pure speculation, with no evidence. Just some guests making guesses over coffee."

The table was starting to fill with other guests, and our conversation switched to photography and scenic sites when Abby came out of the kitchen laden with steaming trays of breakfast.

Valerie Wilson called my cell phone as I was walking back to my room. "Where are you?" I asked, as it was obvious she was talking on a hands-free phone from a moving car.

"Almost there," she said. "Just passed Point Arena. The navigation goodie says seventeen minutes."

"I'll be out in the parking lot," I said. "See you in seventeen minutes."

I went up to my room, and spent way too long trying to make myself look good. I knew it wasn't for Valerie. Maybe I wanted her to make some positive comment when Silvia asked how I was. Like that was going to happen. But I had seen more of Valerie in the hospital when I was recuperating from the bullet wound than I had of Silvia. Valerie was special.

I was out in the parking lot, watching each car drive by on the highway, for a good ten minutes despite my dallying in front of the mirror. Finally, a blue Murano pulled into the driveway, with a small gray-blonde driver, dressed much too well for a vacation on the north coast. Someone might mistake her for a high-end real estate agent, if there was any high-end real estate around here.

"Hey Jimmy," she said, getting out of the car. She gave me a strong sisterly hug. "Sil says hi." She reached in and pulled out a leather briefcase. "She also says you're playing this seat of the pants, and I should expect to either spend the night and come home, or spend a week digging through something messy. So I take it no one is expecting me."

She followed me as I walked slowly towards the reception desk. I was in no hurry, as I wanted to fill her in before she met Abigail McDougal.

"You're a friend who loves the idea of a spontaneous seaside vacation with her old friend Jimmy," I said. "I called you to see if you could help Abigail with the books for the lodge, and you decided to come out for a visit, even if there's nothing to do. I'll spring you on Abby in a few minutes."

She considered this, and stopped walking a few yards from the door to the reception desk.

"That story is a little weak," she said. "Needs some spicing up."

She turned and put her arms around my neck, and gave me a full-on kiss on the lips, complete with one stylish shoe lifted off the ground.

"That should get them talking," she said. She held me at arm's length and regarded my surprised look. "And fun too. Just keep your hands where I can see them. That was just for show." She winked; making sure her admonition was ambiguous.

I recovered gracelessly, and we walked into the empty reception area. I was sure either Gina or Maria, or perhaps both, had been watching us from one of the windows of the lodge, and word would get around that Jimmy's friend was someone close. I started to wish it were true.

As usual, the reception desk was unmanned, and I dragged open the huge door to the bar, and we walked in. Abigail McDougal was behind the bar, her preferred comfort zone, polishing something that was probably already spotless. Valerie placed her arm around my waist as we walked up to the bar.

"Hi Abby," I said, trying to keep a light tone. "This is my friend Valerie Wilson. She's the accountant I told you about, who could help you with your taxes, get the books in shape if you like. When I told her about this place, she couldn't wait to see it, and she just drove right up."

Valerie gave my waist a squeeze, letting Abby know that there might be other reasons for the visit than scenery. Abigail stood behind the bar and regarded us silently. She seemed to be searching for words.

"You were serious," she said, looking around for something else to polish. Not finding anything, she put down the cloth and looked at Valerie. "I can't afford an accountant," she said.

Valerie took up the slack. "I do this for friends for fun all the time. But I'm sensing something here, and I think I know what it is. So I'll tell you what — we start off with me doing it for free. If you like what you get, and you feel you need to compensate me somehow, I'll make you the same deal I pitch to new customers. You can pay me ten percent of whatever I save you over what you paid last year in taxes. But that's totally optional. I really do love what I do for a living. I love helping people out."

Abigail considered this. She picked up the towel and dried her already dry hands. "So you'll clean up the books, and you think you can save me ten times what I pay you, compared to last year."

"Easily," Valerie said. "I'm a pro. And that's without doing anything that will get the IRS bothered. I do this all the time."

"You haven't even seen what you're up against," Abigail warned.

"Give me last year's tax return, and a bucket of receipts, and I'm in heaven," Valerie said.

"Upstairs," Abigail said, pointing to the ceiling. She lifted the bar gate, and Valerie and I slipped under. Abigail led us through a door and up a flight of stairs to a door marked "Office". She unlocked the door, and unclipped the key from a large bundle of keys on a ring and held it in front of Valerie. Valerie took the key and put it into her pocket. We entered the room.

There was a large desk, covered in papers, and three four-drawer filing cabinets against a wall. The window looked out onto the cliffs and the sea, and I could see the parking lot below when I walked closer. A computer screen took up most of the space on the desk, and a keyboard pulled out from a drawer under the desk. Next to the keyboard was taped a three-by-five card with logins and passwords. Abigail pointed to those and said, "All the books are on the computer, those will get you in. If you need help with any of the computer shit, you're on your own — the manuals are on the shelf over there." She pointed to a cluttered bookshelf against the wall opposite the filing cabinets.

Valerie sat down in front of the computer and moved the mouse. The screen lit up a second or two later, showing several windows already open.

"Excellent," Valerie said, moving the mouse to one of the windows. "Let's see what Santa left us." She started clicking on menus, bringing up window after window of financial statements for the lodge.

"Looks like the books usually get done just in time for taxes each year," Valerie said, swiveling around in the chair. "So there's about seven or eight months worth of stuff to load into the program." She swiveled back around and moved some papers on the desk. "You have some bank statements here and bank passwords on the card," she said pointing to the card taped next to the keyboard. "So I can download any that are missing. You really ought to lock that card up somewhere, you know. Maybe get a fireproof safe in here, just a little one, for backups and things like this," she pointed to the card again.

She swiveled the chair around, this time to face me. "That's it for you, Jimmy. This is usually considered private, between the business owner and the accountant. You're going to have to find someplace else to be for a while."

I saluted smartly, and headed for the door. Abigail turned to follow. "You have fun," she said to Valerie. "If you decide to run away screaming, drop the key off down at the bar on your way out."

Abigail led the way back down the stairs. Halfway down, she stopped and turned around. "She staying with you tonight?" she asked.

"Um, no, she'll need her own room," I said.

"Whatever. She can have 204. I'll get you the key."

We continued down the stairs, and Abigail opened a door that led to the reception desk. She pulled out the key to room 204, and handed it to me.

A Quiet Place to Die

"I'll be tending bar if you need anything," she said, and walked back through the door, closing it behind her.

I walked back out into the parking lot, the mid-morning sun feeling good on my back, the sea breeze cold everywhere else. I looked up to find the office window, but I couldn't see Valerie.

At the end of the parking lot, there was a small motorboat on a trailer, hitched to a four-wheel drive truck. I suspected that it belonged to Dave and Janet Hartley, which gave me an idea.

I didn't know which room they were in, but a quick trip to the unattended reception desk allowed me to read the guest ledger. I walked over to room 108 and knocked on the door.

Dave Hartley opened the door. "Mr. Flintstone," he said, smiling. "How can I do you for?"

"I had a question about the local ocean currents. I was wondering if your wife might be able to answer it for me." I looked past him into the room. It was cluttered with equipment; scuba gear, a wetsuit hung on a door to dry, an unfinished painting, and various boxes, knapsacks, and duffle bags. There was barely room to walk.

"Janet!" Hartley called into the bathroom. "The writer guy from breakfast is here, wants to know something about ocean currents."

We waited for an answer for almost a minute. The bathroom door opened, and Janet Hartley came out, dressed in a bikini, toweling her hair dry. "Ocean what?" she said.

"Ocean currents," I answered. "I was wondering if it would be possible to tell where something would end up if I dropped it off the cliff at Pelican Point."

Dave Hartley looked at me, one eyebrow raised slightly. "Something like the guy that went missing there?"

"Exactly," I said. Janet sat down on the bed and continued to towel her head dry. She reached for a hairbrush before answering.

"We could look," she said. "There isn't anything like a map of currents in the area. They'd be all over the place that close to shore. But we can see where the tide was, and the general speed of the currents. They would end up going south of course, on average, no matter what they did locally."

She brushed her hair as she spoke. "Dave, get out my laptop, we can look some things up."

Dave Hartley looked around for the computer, and I watched Janet. She had a plain, almost masculine face, but a figure that most Hollywood actresses would pay good money for, and watching the thin fabric of the bikini move as she stroked her hair was fascinating. Dave cleared some space on the dresser top under the television and set up the computer.

Janet wrapped the towel around her head and walked over to sit in front of the computer. I walked over to look over her shoulder, being careful what I watched, with Dave standing close to me.

It took a few minutes for the computer to come to life, and a bit more for Janet to find what she was looking for. An aerial view of the coast appeared in a window, with small arrows covering the ocean to indicate current direction. "Don't believe the current marks as they get close to the coast," Janet said. "They are pretty much random, and depend a lot on the tide and the wind. The ones farther out are good, though, pretty reliable."

She brought up another window. "What time do you want to drop him in the water?" she asked.

I looked down at her face. The wording of the question had caught me off guard. "Late Monday night," I said. "After ten, maybe as late as midnight."

Janet entered the date and time, then got the longitude and latitude from the ocean current chart, and entered that. The window filled with a tide chart centered on eleven o'clock on Monday night.

"Towards low tide, moving out. He'd hit the rocks and stick. Wouldn't move until the tide came in," she said, scrolling the window down, "maybe five in the morning, or as late as six."

She went back to the aerial view. "Tide coming in, he'd stay close to shore for about five or six hours. Figure a little over half a mile per hour, maybe three and a half miles." She pointed with the mouse on the map.

"Trouble is, it would be moving through kelp, and hitting the shore a lot, since the tide was coming in. I'd bet anything big would get caught in the rocks off the point here. Dave and I found a big dead seal in there last year. It acts like a sieve. And you can't get a boat in there. But you might be able to see it from a hundred yards away or so."

I looked at the map. "How sure are you of all this?" I asked.

"Not sure at all. But the wind would push it there, the currents would push it there, and things get stuck in there for weeks until the crabs and gulls are done with them. It's a big mess of rocks, not exactly a small target." She looked up at me, and I shifted my gaze to her face.

"Sounds like a party," Dave Hartley said loudly. "Want to go check it out?"

"Not me," Janet said. "I'm out of the water for the day. You two have fun though. Fill the outboard first though. Remember that time off Catalina."

"We'll fill it up," Dave said, cutting her off before she could detail the misadventure. He looked at me. "You game? Let's go find a dead guy."

I had planned on phoning the idea in to Corcoran. But Hartley seemed to relish the idea of a boat trip, and maybe a story to tell. He began sorting through the debris on the floor, picking out a duffle bag, an ice chest, and a few other odds and ends. I helped him carry the items out to the pickup truck with the boat trailer.

When we were carrying the second load out to the truck, Randy Hanson was standing by the boat.

"Want to come with us to find the dead guy?" Hartley called out.

Hanson waited until I caught up. "Who is it this time?" he said, shaking his head.

I tossed a duffle bag that must have been full of anchors into the truck bed. "Janet helped figure out where the tides and currents would have taken someone who fell off of Pelican Point. It's a long shot, but there seems to be a pile of rocks that traps things like that. Dave is all gung-ho about it, so I thought what the hell."

Dave was ginning ear to ear. "How about it? Want to come along? Maybe fish some chum out of the water? Great day for a boat ride, eh?"

Hanson needed no further convincing. "Let me go get some camera gear," he said, and ran off towards his car.

I climbed into the back seat of the extended cab, leaving the passenger seat for Hanson when he arrived, carrying a digital SLR in a waterproof housing. He handed it back to me as he got in and slammed the door.

"First stop is for gas for the boat," Hartley said, "so we'll be going way out of our way for a while. Then we'll double back and hit the boat ramp at the cove."

As we drove, I explained the logic Janet had used to make the prediction. She hadn't given odds, but it seemed unlikely to me that we would find anything. Yet the tide and the wind would both have kept a body close to the shore for the first five miles or so, and if it wasn't trapped in the rock sieve, maybe it had washed up somewhere in between. If it hadn't been caught in either place, by now it was likely far out to sea and well down the coast, and unlikely to show up anywhere soon, if ever.

Gas stations are few and far between on the north coast, and it took twenty minutes to find one. Hartley filled the tank in the boat, another five-gallon container strapped in the bed of the truck, and we were off, going back towards Russian Cove.

What Hartley called the boat ramp was actually just a small, unpaved road following the creek at the bottom of a canyon. The creek spilled out into Russian Cove, and the gravel road ended in wet sand near the shore. There was no room to turn the truck around, and Hartley had come in headfirst. I wondered how he was going to back the boat into the water.

He jumped out of the truck and began unfastening the boat from the trailer. Hanson followed, and I crawled out of the back seat to join them. I placed Hanson's camera in the boat.

"You two take that side, I'll take this side, and we'll lift it out and carry it to the beach," Hartley instructed. He lifted his side a few inches, and Hanson and I took hold of our side and heaved.

The little boat was amazingly heavy, and I gained new respect for the younger man holding up his end all by himself. He splashed through the creek in his running shoes, while Hanson and I stayed on the high ground. By the time the boat was at the beach, its back end floating as six inch high waves lifted it, I was breathing heavily, and setting the load down caused my arms and back to feel weightless, as if I was about to leave the ground.

Hartley walked back to the truck to get more gear, and Hanson and I followed. Hanson seemed to be as relieved as I was that our short exertion was over, but I noticed he was walking faster than I was. He grabbed the heavy duffle, and I took the ice chest. Hartley made one trip with the rest, loaded on his arms as on a forklift.

Hartley shoved the boat farther out into the water, and Hanson and I got in, moving to the rear, where the boat was already floating. Our weight changed that, but Hartley still managed to push the boat off the sand until it was fully floating, and splashed into knee-deep water before jumping in.

We changed places awkwardly, rocking the little boat as it drifted farther from the shore. Hartley tugged at the outboard and fiddled with the choke until eventually the engine caught and the water under the boat made a burbling sound. He engaged the prop, and we headed out of the cove into the rolling swells.

Cold spray hit my face as we hit wave after wave in the little boat, banging into each one with a shudder. I moved closer to the center of the boat to escape the spray, and sat down on the small bench in the center, trying to present as little of my body to the wind as possible. The noon sun seemed incapable of warming, being late October low in the southern sky.

Eventually we were far enough out of the cove that Hartley could turn the boat north around the point. The waves no longer perpendicular to our path, the slamming of the boat transformed into a slow ride up the swell, and a slow ride back down, each time tipping the little boat first to one side then the other. The spray ceased to be a problem, but the roll was affecting my stomach. I looked out to the shore to anchor my sense of motion, and gradually the urge to lose breakfast passed.

Hanson was already taking pictures. The cliffs were sunlit from this angle, and what shadows there were showed a deep black, with no sense of anything contained within. The boat seemed to make only the tiniest bit of progress as I watched the shore. I got the sense that I could have walked on the beach faster than we were traveling. Watching kelp and bubbles pass the boat, I got the opposite impression; that I could not have run as fast as the boat was moving. I imagined reality to be somewhere between the two.

It was at least an hour before we were close to the rock pile that Janet had pointed out on the map. Waves crashed on it and sent plumes of spray into the air, and sea birds wheeled in the air and screeched at the waves. Hanson snapped away with the camera, and Hartley brought the little boat dangerously close to the rocks. We all scanned for any sign of something caught in the rocks, but from this southern angle, it was unlikely that we would see anything brought to the rocks from the north.

The little boat fought through the swells as Hartley turned out to sea again to get around the rocks, and the slamming of the bow resumed. My polarized sunglasses cut through the glare of the reflected cliffs in the water, and I searched every rock for something that didn't belong.

The boat turned north again, and we could gradually see more and more of the rock pile. Gulls were diving and calling in the wind, and still there was no sign that the rocks held anything of any interest to our small party. The tide was ebbing from the high just before nine, and would be lowest about twenty minutes to four in the afternoon, according to Janet. My watch said one thirty, so we had two hours before the full low tide. If the body was wedged deep in the rocks, that would be the best time to look.

Beyond the rock pile was a small sliver of sandy beach, pressed up close to the edge of the cliff. Hartley aimed the boat in that direction, and we continued to scan the rocks as we approached it. When the small boat finally crunched up onto the sand and Hartley cut the engine, the relative silence of the waves slapping at the little beach was a relief. We jumped off the bow as the last wave retreated, and hurried to pull the boat up on the beach, helped by the next wave.

"There comes a time in a man's life," Hartley said, "when it's time for a beer." He pulled out the heavy duffle bag, which turned out to be filled not with anchors, but with cans of imported beer. The beer was cold, despite not having been transferred to the ice chest, and we stood in silence for a moment as we drank.

The little beach ended at the pile of rocks, and we started over in that direction, looking for any signs of Gill Barnett. With the drier rocks we could jump from one to another, but as we got closer to the waves, the going became tedious, and the rocks slippery. I checked every crevice I could see, and slowly moved farther out into the spray. Hanson stayed closer to the cliff, taking picture after picture, trying to get a high angle to see into pools between the rocks. Dave Hartley was having a great time scrambling over rocks slick with algae and seaweed, or crusted with barnacles, limpets, and mussels. He was getting soaked, but didn't seem to care.

I found a large rock with a flat top, and climbed up to get a higher view. I picked up a kelp float, tugged off the leaf, and threw the float as far as I could into the water north of the rocks. I watched for several minutes as the float slowly drifted with the wind, the waves, and the current. Judging by its progress, if we were going to find anything, it would be farther out in the rocks, amid the crashing waves.

We climbed around the rocks for an hour and a half, and the tide was nearly at its lowest point. Still, we had seen no indication that we were in the right place, or lucky. I was exhausted, Hanson looked little better, but Dave Hartley was still jumping from rock to rock like the small shorebirds he frightened as he approached.

Finally, though, even Hartley agreed that we had done as much searching as we could on foot, and we made our way back to the boat, now firmly high and dry at low tide. We pushed it back out into the water, none of us any longer worried about getting our feet wetter than they already were, and jumped aboard. Hartley tugged at the outboard a few times, again adjusting the choke, and finally the engine coughed to life. We headed north, scanning the smaller piles of rocks.

In another twenty minutes, we were below Pelican Point, although from our angle we could not see even the guardrail at the edge of the cliff. The rocks below were exposed and dry, and anyone falling from that height would stop very suddenly. Hartley turned the boat back south, and we started home.

Hanson had put down his camera, and was holding tightly to the bow line, feet spread far apart, leaning back, so he had a tripod stance that allowed him to stand up in the small rocking boat. He scanned the rocks from this vantage point as we approached the big rock pile again.

I had known the odds were against us when we set out, and had been running mostly on Dave Hartley's enthusiasm. So it was a complete surprise to me when Hanson yelled out.

"Over there!" he said, pointing into the rocks, now exposed much more now that the tide was completely out. I looked in the direction he was pointing, and saw a crowd of sea gulls clustering around an object wedged into the rocks. It was white and blue, and could very well be jeans and a T-shirt.

"Hand me the camera," he shouted, holding onto the bow line with one hand, and reaching back towards me with the other. I passed him the camera, and he held it high over his head, not looking through the viewfinder or at the screen, just taking shot after shot as the boat rode over swells and rocked back and forth.

Hartley circled the boat around, trying to keep enough distance from the rocks while still keeping control of the boat. I kept looking at the object, trying to estimate the size. It looked small, but it could have been that most of the body was still wedged between the rocks.

I made a decision, and pulled my cell phone out of my pocket. There was enough here to warrant a closer look, and there was no way we could get any closer in the little boat. I searched for the sheriff's number, and pressed the button to dial. The noise of the surf and the engine made it hard to hear, and I could not tell if anyone had answered. Then I looked more closely at the phone.

"No signal," I shouted to Hartley, showing him the phone. "Can't call the sheriff."

"We'll go back in then," he shouted. "Call from the lodge."

It took nearly an hour to get the boat back to Russian Cove and loaded onto the trailer. Hartley backed the trailer up the dirt road, occasionally moving forward to straighten out the trailer, and then back up the road again. It was slow going, and Hanson got out when we got to the highway so he could watch for cars as Hartley backed the trailer out onto the pavement, and then quickly forward, pulling as far to the side of the road as he could. Hanson ran back to the truck and jumped in, and we started back to the lodge.

My cell phone kept going in and out of service as the road wound and dipped, and I gave up on trying to use it. When we finally pulled into the driveway of the lodge, we all climbed out and made quickly for the reception desk.

Now at the top of the cliff, my phone had a signal again, but I was tempted to use the phone at the desk anyway. Laziness eventually took hold, and I pressed the redial button instead.

"Sheriff's office," came the now familiar voice.

"Tell Gabe Corcoran we've found Gill Barnett's body in the rocks about five miles south of Pelican Point. We can't reach it by foot or by boat. He may want to call the Coast Guard for a search and rescue chopper."

"The deputy isn't here right now," said the voice.

"Then find him. But call the Coast Guard in the meantime, because the tide is going to come back up, and every hour is going to make it that much harder to pull the body out of the rocks."

"Do you have the number for the Coast Guard?" came the voice.

"Check your damned speed dial!" I shouted into the phone. "And find Corcoran. Have him call this number right away."

"Ok," came the voice, still calm and unperturbed by my cursing rant. "Is there anything else you require?"

"Just get the deputy and the Coast Guard. I can handle the rest," I said.

I snapped the phone closed with a loud clap and put it back into my pocket. Dave Hartley ran back to his room to tell Janet the news. Hanson and I squished in our wet shoes into the bar, to see if anyone was there. Abigail McDougal was behind the bar, and George Franco was nursing a beer, watching a football game.

"We found Gill Barnett," Hanson said to Abigail. She looked up at us. "On the rocks, about two miles south of here. We couldn't get to the body."

"You sure it was Gill?" she asked.

"We won't know until the Coast Guard can pull him out of the rocks," I said. "It could be just a pair of jeans and a T-shirt, but something is keeping them together and inflated."

Abigail looked uncertain.

"Think I should call Catherine?" she asked softly.

"Let's wait on that. Until the sheriff's department is sure. That could be real hard to handle," I said. I had always hated making those calls when I was with the department.

"We called the sheriff," Hanson offered. "But he wasn't there. Just some clown who didn't know the number for the Coast Guard." He smiled at me as he said that, and pulled out a chair to sit down at a table. I pulled out another chair, and sat down, my wet jeans making a squishing sound on the chair.

Abigail looked at the clock. "I'll call Rosie's. He stops in there for pie most days. He's probably still there, the old lard-butt."

She punched the number into the phone behind the bar. Hanson looked down at his wet shoes, and the small puddle we were making under the table. I had sand in the toes of my shoes, and I could feel it shift when I wiggled them.

"Hi there, Joss," Abigail said into the phone. "Is Gabe Corcoran there? Yeah, could you tell him to get his ass over to McDougal's? Someone's found a floater, washed up on the rocks 'tween here and the cove. Blue jeans and a T-shirt could be Gill Barnett. Yeah, tell him that. He's going to need the Coast Guard I hear, so have him call them too."

She hung up the phone, and walked away from the bar, through the door that led to the office stairs. She came back out, holding a mop, and she thrust it towards me.

"Clean up that mess," she said, pointing to the puddle under the table, "and then go shower and change. Gabe won't get here for twenty minutes, max."

She lifted the bar gate and went back to her station. George Franco continued to watch the football game, apparently unaware that anyone else was in the bar. He probably hadn't heard a thing we had said.

Hanson moved chairs while I mopped, and I put the mop back behind the bar. We walked out, shoes squishing. I ignored the small trail of droplets that followed us out the door.

Later, showered and changed, I felt much better. I had only brought one pair of shoes, however, so I walked back to the parking lot barefoot. Dave Hartley was there, with Hanson and Janet. Hanson had not bothered to change, but Hartley was wearing a pair of swimming trunks, his hair wet from a quick shower.

"It was right where she said it would be, wasn't it," Hartley shouted when he saw me. I nodded and approached the group.

"It was a big pile of rocks," I said. "Good call on that. I never thought we'd find anything."

Janet looked at her husband, who was still triumphantly grinning. "Frankly, neither did I," she said.

We were halfway through describing the trip and the location when Corcoran arrived. He did not seem pleased to see me at all.

"What's this about a body?" he said, adjusting his belt. He walked up to me, ignoring the rest of the group.

"We took a boat trip out to a big bunch of rocks a couple miles south of here," I said. "Janet here is a scientist, and she told us where to look. We found him right at low tide, so if someone is going to get him out of the rocks, they'd better be quick. The tide is coming back in."

"Search and rescue already got the call from Charlie at the station," Corcoran said, making a face like he'd just eaten a bug. "There better damn well be something out there, or I'm going to make your people pay the bill."

A Quiet Place to Die

I ignored the comment. "Janet has a map of the area. I can point out the exact location, and we can get the GPS coordinates for the chopper."

Janet nodded, and started walking back to her room. The rest of us followed, Corcoran bringing up the rear.

"I took a sighting from the edge of Pelican Point to the white house on the hill here," I said, pointing to the aerial photo. "So that would make a line going this way." I moved my finger along the screen, tracing a line from the white splotch through Pelican Point and out to sea.

"I took another sight down this way, where the point north of the cove met up with the rock fall over here," I said, tracing another line out to sea. "So where the two lines cross, that's where we saw the body."

I pointed to the spot on the screen. There were no rocks in the photo, so it must not have been taken at low tide. "Right here," I said, taking the mouse from Janet, and moving the cursor to the point. "Can we find out what the latitude and longitude are for that spot?"

Janet pulled up another map, and moved the mouse to the equivalent spot. She read off the numbers from the screen, and I entered them in my phone. Corcoran was writing them on a pad he had extracted from his utility belt. He went back out to his car to use the radio.

Hanson had opened his camera and pulled out the memory chip. "Can we pull these up on the computer? I took a lot of shots with the telephoto. It's image stabilized, and the exposure was short, but we might still have too much motion blur. The boat was moving around a lot."

Janet inserted the chip into a slot in the front of the laptop, and copied the photos onto her disk. It took a long time, as the photos were large, and Hanson had snapped hundreds of them. He scanned the thumbnails until he found the group he had shot after spotting the body.

Several of the photos were indeed too blurry to see anything. But most were sharp and clear. He zoomed in on the blue and white spot caught in the rocks, until we could see individual pixels on the screen.

"I don't think that's a T-shirt," Janet said, pointing to the white spot. "That's someone's back. That spot looks like a tattoo. He's all white from being in the water for two days. That's definitely blue jeans. That white spot is a foot."

We looked at several of the photos, and Hanson cropped out the body from a set of clear shots, all from slightly different directions, and arrayed them on the screen. We were definitely looking at a body.

"Can you email those to me?" I said, handing Hanson my business card.

Outside, we could hear the sound of a helicopter in the distance, out to sea. I went out to stand with Corcoran, who was holding the radio mike in his hand.

"They see it," he said. "They're going to lower some poor slob down with a rescue basket. If they just tie a rope to it, all they're gonna get is pieces."

The rest of our group had come out again, and Dave Hartley was standing on the roof of his truck, trying to see down over the cliff. He was not successful. All of the action was hidden from view. He got in the truck and drove off to find a better sightseeing spot.

Our little crowd was getting larger. Gina Franco and Maria the maid had come out, and so had a couple of guests I had not yet met. I tried to make out words in the scratchy noise from Corcoran's radio. Minutes dragged by. Janet had brought out the laptop computer, and was showing the photos to the newcomers.

Half an hour had gone by, and the group was noticeably smaller when a squawk on the radio woke Corcoran from some daydream of competence. "They got him," he said, picking the mike up to hold to his face. "No, straight to the EMS morgue manager. I'll meet you there," he said into the mike. "And Charlie, get the triage leader on the horn, I want him present when I get there."

The deputy struggled into the car, pulled the seat belt over his wide girth, and fumbled for the latch. Once belted, he slammed the door and headed for the highway, putting lights and siren on once he was on the public road. I guess I hadn't expected a goodbye, or thanks.

The sun was getting close to the horizon, and the air was beginning to chill. I followed Hanson into the bar. Gina, George, Janet, and most of the group that had been outside trying to see the helicopter were already inside. I walked up to Abigail where she stood behind the bar.

"Already heard all about it," she said, filling a pitcher with beer.

"How's Valerie doing on the books?" I asked.

"Don't know," she said. "Hasn't come down yet."

I pointed to the door and made my face into a question, beginning to lift the bar gate. Abigail shrugged, mocking my silent request for permission. I slid under the bar gate and went through the door, and upstairs to the office.

I knocked on the closed door. Valerie opened it a crack, and seeing me, opened it all the way.

"Come on in. I almost have the data entry part finished," she said.

"We found Gill Barnett's body," I said. "Washed into some rocks about five miles south of where he went in."

Valerie screwed up her face, imagining the details of a body bashing against rocks for two days.

"The Coast Guard did the extraction," I said. "We couldn't get close, either by land or in the boat."

"Is he still the prime suspect in McDougal's death?" she asked quietly, not wanting her voice to carry downstairs, despite the closed door.

"He was dodgy on his whereabouts. That's what excited Lee. But we have two more suspects who just lost their alibis, and the lady downstairs may have had motive and opportunity."

"Abby?" Valerie seemed surprised.

"You tell me," I said. "She gets this place, she might get the insurance if it isn't ruled a suicide. Is there enough value in the business for murder?"

She turned around to face the computer. "There's no mortgage. The place is paid off. I haven't tried to run any comps, and that's going to be difficult anyway, since there aren't any. I don't have cash flow numbers yet, but the guest counts up until September were pretty good. I'd guess she's into a couple million here, maybe twice that. I'll have a better idea in a day or two."

I stepped over to look at the screen over her shoulder. Nothing there made sense to me. I was no accountant or businessman.

"I'm also working on whether she might have found him with a bag on his head, and hid the suicide evidence."

She slid the chair back and looked up at me. "That'd be a bitch to prove," she said.

I shrugged. "I signed up for two murders. Now we have three. I should renegotiate."

"You're working this latest? The guy in the water?"

"I found him. But hell, he *was* a suspect, and still is. All this shit is related. And I still haven't got up the nerve to interview the person I think was with him on that cliff." I sat down on the desk, one knee up, pointing towards Valerie.

She leaned forward. "The woman with the fancy shoes."

I nodded. "The singer. Of course, it could be his wife, or some stranger, but the tire prints look right. No word from Corcoran on that, I'll have to have Silvia run a match for me."

Downstairs, I could hear the crowd in the bar getting noisier. I looked at my watch. "And the band should be arriving any minute. Time to catch a singer."

Valerie stood up. "Is she pretty?"

"The singer?" I said. "She's gorgeous. Why?"

"Sil says you never suspect the pretty ones," she said, reaching over to put the computer to sleep.

"That was one case," I said, defensively. Valerie didn't answer. She walked over to open the door, her hand on the light switch. The noise from downstairs got louder as the door opened. I walked out, and Valerie followed, turning off the light, and locking the door behind us.

Downstairs, the crowd was noisy, and Abigail was busy. Valerie held the key up in the air, offering it back to Abby, but Abby waved her off. Valerie placed the key in her purse.

Randy Hanson walked up to us, beer in hand. "No band tonight," he said. "Word got around about the body, and they cancelled."

I didn't mention that Penelope Dixon had been dating a married man. Hanson had already mentioned seeing Barnett and Dixon leave together the night Danny McDougal died. Perhaps he already suspected.

I introduced Randy to Valerie. "I have a question for you," I said to him. "Does Abigail McDougal have a little sister? About four years old?"

Hanson tipped his head sideways, as if the question had been asked of a dog. "The guy was seventy something. He definitely liked the ladies, but the ones that liked him back probably didn't have to worry about birth control anymore. Where did that one come from?"

I tossed off the suggestion with a shrug. "Just something someone said. I probably heard it wrong, or misunderstood."

"Some day, eh?" he said, raising his beer in a toast.

"That it was," I said.

Dave Hartley was standing by a large group of people, telling the story of the afternoon again. He was probably getting pretty good at it by now. He was enjoying himself. Hanson left to join the group. I pulled Valerie off to the side where we could speak in private.

"McDougal had a teddy bear with him when he died. In a gift box for a birthday party. He told the clerk at the store it was for his four-year-old daughter. Not niece, not granddaughter, not someone else's daughter. I need you to look for anything that might indicate other family members. Payments for child support, any big expenses four years before the day he died, like to a hospital, or anything that looks like it might be for a girlfriend with a four-year-old kid. And don't ask about it, just look in the records. I have to be very careful how I ask about things like that."

Valerie nodded. "There are a number of ways things like that would show up. But I have access to his personal bank account, as well as the business account. All the passwords are on the card at the desk, and I emailed myself a photo of the card with my phone, just in case we need them."

I leaned back against one of the tables. "You should delete that. It's illegal to log in unless it's directly related to work the client has asked you to do. I'm just saying that in the course of tidying up the books; keep a lookout for anything that could tell us how to find the little girl he was bringing the teddy bear to. Her name is Sarah. I don't have a last name."

Valerie shrugged off my admonition. "This is a lady on your list as a murder suspect. Someone who may have killed her own father.

A Quiet Place to Die

And may have killed Lee Aleada. And may have pushed some poor guy off a cliff. What if there's something in the bank account that proves she's a killer?"

I shook my head. "Then find some reason why you need to look there to tidy the books. Get permission. This needs to be strictly legal, especially if we're going to court with what we find. And you don't want to end up in court on the wrong side."

She still wasn't buying my argument. "You're soft on her, *aren't you?*"

I shook my head. "And make sure she changes those passwords when you're done, and doesn't keep the new ones taped to the computer desk."

Until proven otherwise, everyone is innocent. If I didn't believe that, I couldn't do what I do. I need to make friends with all the people who can help me figure this out. They need to trust me, and they can't if I don't trust them. I hold onto every spec of doubt, cling to it, so I can make friends with people who might have done very bad things. Because there are a lot more good guys than bad guys. That's how I sleep at night.

I spent the rest of the evening taking photos of Valerie. I had her pose wherever there was a face in the background I wanted a photo of. It's an old trick, but so far, no one has caught on. I use it a lot. My memory needs all the help I can get. Besides, when a body is found, the killer will often want to know what's being said. I paid close attention to anyone who seemed particularly interested in what Dave Hartley was saying. Unfortunately, that was just about everyone.

Everyone, that is, except Abigail McDougal. She filled beer mugs and cocktail glasses with the same disinterest she had shown in all things all week. Did standing out make her more of a suspect? What had killed both curiosity and sociability in this young woman? I could not tell guilt from child abuse, and that bothered me.

It was late when we left the bar. I pulled the key to room 204 out of my pocket and handed it to Valerie as we climbed the stairs.

"Which one's your room?" she asked, taking the key.

"Right next door. Let's see — don't feed the raccoons, breakfast is between seven and ten, there's more wood for the fire but you won't need it because they top it off every morning. And you won't need an alarm clock. The blue jays will make sure you're awake." We got to my room. I pointed to her door.

"What, you're not going to tuck me in?" she said playfully.

"You're really milking this cover story thing," I said.

"We're not that old, Jimmy. Have a little fun," she said.

"What, mix business with pleasure?" I asked.

"You remember what the hooker said to the vicar, don't you?" She turned her key in the lock of 204.

"Do I want to know?" I asked.

"It's a business doing pleasure with you," she said, and walked through the door without another word.

In my room, I went to the computer and detailed the last two days into an email addressed to Silvia and Corcoran. I left out a few little things, but I made sure to ask about the tire tread match.

In a separate note to Silvia alone, I asked her to research births on September 29th, four years ago, in a hundred mile radius, looking for a baby named Sarah.

§

Hack Hartley

The blue jays had yet to arrive at my window when I was awakened by a knock on the door.

I sat up in bed and rubbed my eyes. The knock came again. It did not come from the door I had come in, but seemed instead to come from the closet.

I got out of bed, and pulled on my pants. I went to the closet door, which was locked. I unlocked the door, and opened it to find Valerie standing behind another open door, in her room.

"Why did you lock your side?" she asked. "Afraid I'd sneak in and rape you in the middle of the night?"

The two open doors now connected the two adjoining rooms. Of course, there hadn't been two closets in my room. I might have felt sheepish about not noticing if I hadn't still been half-asleep.

Valerie was looking at the circular scar on my shoulder. She reached her hand out to touch it. "I remember that one," she said, walking around me to see the much less symmetrical exit wound scar. "She was one of the pretty ones. You're lucky it was a twenty-two, Jimmy. You really can't trust the pretty ones."

I yawned and walked into the bathroom. "I'm going to have a nice long hot shower," I said. "If I fall asleep in here, don't wake me up."

"Where's breakfast?" she called through the door I had just closed.

"In the lodge, turn left. It's opposite the door to the bar. And don't let Gina Franco pump you when I'm not there, you'll screw up the cover story."

I didn't hear her leave, as I had the shower running. I didn't hurry. I like long hot showers. Some of my best thinking happens there. If I'm awake.

After the shower, I dressed, and the blue jays fought over who got to scold me for spoiling the fun of waking me. I yawned again, and closed the door to Valerie's room, then walked my door to greet the cold predawn dampness of the north coast in October. It wasn't even seven o'clock yet.

Someone had placed small pumpkins outside every door, and on the corners of the railings. I wondered how long the Halloween decorations would last if raccoons found out they were edible. There were ears of Indian corn, still on tall stalks, decorating the corners of each building.

I walked out into the light fog, trying to remember when the sun rose. Sometime soon. Before seven, at least. At the reception desk there was a poster detailing events leading up to Halloween. Tonight was billed as the Vampire's Ball, costumes optional. I imagined all the guests dancing naked. I stopped when the image of Gina Franco dancing in the nude nearly had me laughing out loud.

Valerie had set up her laptop computer at a small table in a corner, near a wall socket. No one else was in the room – we had even beaten Gina and George to breakfast.

I walked over to Valerie's table. "We'll be sitting with the group," I said. "Or at least I will." I didn't want to sound pushy. She didn't seem to care.

"I'll be done with my email in a minute. Can I get some coffee somewhere?" she asked.

"I think Abby makes it the night before and microwaves it when she gets to the kitchen. It's kind of chewy. And she probably isn't out of bed yet." A sound from behind the door leading to the kitchen called me a liar.

"Caffeine in any form will do," she said.

On cue, Abigail McDougal came through the door, carrying coffee and cups on a tray. She looked up at us, momentarily confused at the seating. I walked to the large table, and she set down the tray there.

"Good morning, Abby," I said.

"So far," she replied.

I waited for some sign she was joking. It didn't come. Before she could leave, I jumped in with a question.

"Do you know a little girl, about four years old? Named Sarah?"

"No little kids here this week. Month. At least." She turned away and went back through the kitchen door, which swung quietly shut on its pneumatic spring. There had been no recognition on her face, no pause in her answer, nothing. She didn't know any four-year-old girls.

Gina Franco came into the room just as I was sitting down. "Your girlfriend isn't joining us?" she said, pointing to Valerie. I stood up, and took a cup from the tray, acting the gallant boyfriend carrying caffeine to the sleep deprived.

"She will — she's just finishing up some email," I said, walking away with the coffee.

I placed the coffee beside Valerie's laptop. "Oh, thank you, honey," she said, putting her hand on mine and squeezing gently. I grimaced in her direction and walked back to the big table, just as George Franco entered the room.

"Not going to sell a lot of real estate pulling dead bodies out of the water," he said, pulling out a chair beside me, opposite his wife.

"Wouldn't have happened without Dave and Randy," I said. "Dave had the boat; Randy was the one who spotted it."

"Right where his wife predicted it would be," Gina insisted.

"Exactly. I was just along for the ride," I said.

Valerie joined us, trailing the cord to her charger. "Hi there! You must be Gina and George, the ones who keep Jimmy company in the mornings."

And they were off. Gina loved to talk, and Valerie kept her talking, always asking questions that would stimulate Gina's output without stimulating her curiosity. I kept an ear open for any modifications to our cover, but Valerie showed herself to be quite skillful.

Randy Hanson came in and sat down across from me. "Busy day yesterday," he said. "Going to relax a bit today?"

He looked like that was his plan, but the early breakfast said otherwise. "I'm heading up to Pine Grove and Caspar today, then down south. Basically bar hopping. You know," I said, "research".

George Franco laughed loudly at this. "Nice work if you can get it," he said.

Dave Hartley and Janet came in, also unusually early for them. Dave pulled out a chair and spun it around backwards, sitting in it with his hands on the backrest. "Did we kick ass yesterday, or what? I'll bet we really pissed of the sheriff's department, finding him first. They should have been handing out medals, but that deputy looked like we'd pissed on his birthday cake." Dave was enormously pleased with himself, and wore a huge grin.

"Right where you said it would be," Gina said loudly to Janet.

"A job well done, all around," I said, raising my coffee cup in half toast, half salute. The others lifted theirs.

Valerie looked over at Gina. "So, it looks like there's some sort of dance going on tonight?"

Gina was anxious to fill in the details. "The last two weeks of October, they always have something going on every day. It's like a big long Halloween thing. Usually this place is crammed full of tourists here to catch salmon or abalone, but they banned salmon fishing this year, and some people are saying they might ban it next year too, since one year isn't enough to get the salmon population back up where they want it. But still, it's a big deal here, every year. You don't find anything like it anywhere else on the coast."

She took a big gasping breath and began to describe their previous visits at this time of year, and what to expect in the next few days. Abigail brought out breakfast, and I finished mine while Gina was still talking as fast as she could.

Hanson leaned towards me to speak softly without interrupting the torrent. "So, will you be needing any help on your research today?" Hartley leaned in to hear my answer.

"My part will be pretty boring," I said. "A lot of driving and a lot of talking to people who don't know anything. That part works best when I'm alone," I said. I watched their crestfallen faces as they slid back into their chairs.

"But there is something you could do while I'm out that would help," I said. "I took a lot of shots of Valerie last night, and there were a bunch of people in the background that I don't have names for. Usually, I like to get releases from anybody who is in a picture that might get published. That makes an easy cover for getting names matched to suspects, I mean people, who attend large gatherings after an event like what we had yesterday."

Dave Hartley was excited again. "That is so cool! We go around and ask people who the faces in the photos belong to, and we find the perps, and everybody thinks it's to get their name in the paper. That is just brilliant!"

"I'm in," Hanson said. "I may be able to fill in a bunch of names right away. I'm here a lot. We can ask Maria to help, she probably can match the guests with their room numbers, and we can sneak a peek at the registry book to get the names."

That at least would keep them from accompanying me today. And that was good, because what I was about to do might be dangerous. But also, I find people open up better one-on-one than when talking to two or three strangers at the same time.

There are various ways to get strangers to open up to you in a bar. Most of those take time, however. But one way that often works for me is to piss off people with short fuses. It's fast, and if you chose your words carefully, you can home in on what pisses them off the most. If that has something to do with guilt over a recent incident, you get a lot of information with each black eye and fat lip. The downside is the facial damage. That's why I try not to use that method if I can.

If some bikers from up north were in Russian Cove on the night Lee Aleada was murdered, a fat lip might be the only way I was going to find out. But I'd be carrying my gun, to make sure the fat lip and a clue was all I got.

I excused myself, and Hanson and Hartley stood up to follow me. "You have a laptop in your room, don't you?" I asked Hartley, as if I'd forgotten the computer that helped find Gil Barnett. I started walking towards room 108. "We can load the pictures onto it, and you can make notes on it, and show the photos to Maria or the other guests."

"Sounds like a plan," Hartley said, rushing ahead to open the door.

There were a lot of photos. We loaded them onto the computer in impatient silence. Finally, they were all loaded, and Hartley brought up the first one.

"There are George and Gina, and Abby," said Hanson. The two of them quickly named several faces in the background, and two that were unknown. They moved on to the second one.

"I'll leave you two to that," I said. "I have a lot of driving to do."

I went upstairs to my room. From my suitcase, I took out my shoulder holster and put it on, covering it with a light jacket. I also took out the SLR camera and the big zoom lens, and the laptop computer, and then headed out to my car.

In the car, I plugged the laptop's car charger into the cigarette lighter, and plugged in the GPS module. I brought up a map of the local area and set the GPS to record my route. All set up, I headed north.

Bar hopping in the morning is seldom a fruitful activity. But getting away from the chitchat and driving alone were both good enhancers for my cognitive abilities. I would drive around, scout out all the possible biker hangouts, and take some photos of anything I found that was interesting, but mostly I was going to think. And wait for late afternoon. Maybe take a nap.

There isn't much between Russian Cove and Mendocino. But it takes a long time to get there, so you see a lot of it. Roads have extremely creative names like Little River and Big River and Little Lake. That is often an indication that they were not named by people trying to sell real estate. The sparse population of the area confirmed that not a lot of real estate was being sold.

When I got to Mendocino, I drove by the shop where Danny McDougal bought the teddy bear, and took some shots from across the street with the big lens. Something to put in a report. Get to play with the fun toy. I had already thoroughly explored the tiny town. I headed east on Little Lake Road for half an hour, killing time, trying to find a little lake, but there was no sign of it. I headed back.

I got back to Mendocino and headed north. Pine Grove was not far, and I scoured it thoroughly, looking for anything remotely like a biker bar. There was nothing. I didn't even see a motorcycle the whole time I was there.

Caspar was no better. There could not have been more than a couple hundred buildings in the whole place. Anyone wanting nightlife would head north for Fort Bragg. I was beginning to wonder why Randy Hanson had picked these two marks on the map for his biker fantasy.

I continued north, not finding anything that looked the least bit threatening. I did see one motorcycle on the road. The driver was wearing an expensive unscratched helmet, and a tan fringed jacket, and she looked quite nice, but hardly threatening.

I gave up on Hanson's fantasies, and stopped for a late lunch in Fort Bragg. Why would Hanson want to make up a story blaming vague outsiders from towns he had apparently never actually visited? I could think of no motives for his involvement in any of the murders. Was he protecting someone? Did he suspect a friend? How many friends did he have in Russian Cove? I counted Rafe, Gill, Johnny Mac, Abigail, and then finally Jennifer Strike before I got to someone that wasn't on my own list of possibilities.

I paid for lunch and started driving south. It was a little after two o'clock, and it took me over an hour and a half to get to Gualala, where Hack Hartley's bar was supposed to be. Aleada had not logged exact GPS coordinates, or even an address, so I had to cruise around looking for it. It was after four o'clock when I found the neon sign that said "Hartley's". And I had finally found some motorcycles, arranged neatly next to five parked cars. Quite a lot of business for a Thursday afternoon. I parked in one of three remaining spots, and walked up to the open door.

A poster by the door read "Cross Dance Tonight!", and I could hear music and voices inside. I walked in the door and let my eyes adjust to the dim lighting. There was a bar on the left, a stage on the right, and a jukebox at the far end of the room. Six small round tables with four chairs each stood between me and the jukebox, and three of them were occupied. Two men were seated at the bar. On the stage, and attractive petite dancer was fondling a stripper's pole, playfully lifting a short skirt. The makeup was almost hiding his five o'clock shadow.

Every eye in the place was following me as I walked over and sat down at the bar. The other two at the bar were dressed in black leather sleeveless vests and leather pants, and huge muscles bulged on their arms. A lot of gym work was involved in keeping up those physiques. The bartender was also a gym fanatic, perhaps not as much as the two at the bar, but he would stand out at a Safeway, if not at Gold's Gym. I pointed to the tap. "I'd like a beer," I said to the bartender. He stepped closer.

"Any particular brand of beer?" he said.

A Quiet Place to Die

"I'm into surprises," I said, and this generated a snort of laughter from the leather-clad man farthest from me at the bar. The bartender's expression did not change, and he poured me a beer from the tap. I recognized the bartender's face from Aleada's file photos.

"Hartley," I said, noticing a pause in his step when I said the name. "Do you know a Dave Hartley, does paintings of the coast around here?" The question fell dead in the air. I thought for a moment that I was being ignored.

"Lot of Hartleys," the bartender said.

"He's up at Russian Cove," I said, "staying at McDougal's. He and I fished a dead guy out of the water yesterday; maybe it made the news down here. Guy named Gill Barnett."

The big man stopped walking away and turned around to look at me. He seemed to consider several possible things to say, and discarded each one in turn. Finally, he decided on something.

"What brings you down here?" he said.

I let a pause develop, and watched his face. When the pause would have been uncomfortable for most people, his face remained stoic. "Thirst?" I said, breaking the tension.

Again the snort from the biker at the bar.

"You a cop?" the Hack Hartley asked. This time I answered right away.

"Newspaper reporter. Freelance. Mostly small stuff, local papers, that kind of thing. You may have seen my stuff," I said, and looked around at the patrons in the bar. "Or maybe not. Name's Jimmy Davis." I held out my hand. Hartley ignored it.

"What are you doing *here*?" Hartley asked again. I was definitely getting a sense of menace from the tone of voice. The two bikers at the bar sat up straighter, if that is a word I could use in this context.

"You don't know Dave Hartley," I said. "That's too bad, he's a great guy, you'd like him. You could put one of his paintings up over the bar there. How about some other guys from up there? Like Rafael Gonzales?" I said, watching the man's face for a sign of recognition. A slight tightening of the crow's feet at the corners of his eyes. A slight pause in his breathing. "Or Johnny McCarthy?"

This last caused a stir of movement from the bar patrons, and the same tightening around the eyes for Hack Hartley. He considered what he was going to say next.

"Perhaps you want to finish your beer," he said.

I ignored the comment. "Johnny Mac, now there's a character. He and Rafe, they're like this," I said, putting my index fingers tightly together, side by side. "And Gill Barnett, until the other day. You know that makes three people dead in just a couple of weeks? That must be some kind of record for a quiet little place like this. What do you think the county gets in an average year, four, maybe five murders tops?"

As I spoke, the biker nearest me stood up and walked behind me. I stopped talking when a firm hand fell on my shoulder, pushing me down into the seat. His other hand reached into my back pocket, and pulled out my wallet, which he handed to the bartender. Hack Hartley opened the wallet as the biker behind me placed his free hand on my other shoulder. His friend was also standing.

"James Willoughby Davis," Hartley read from my driver's license. He pulled out credit cards, auto insurance card, dental insurance card, and a Kaiser Permanente card from the wallet and laid them out on the table. The small stack of business cards followed them.

"Freelance journalist," he read from a card. He put the card into his shirt pocket.

"Let me give you some free advice," he said, his voice low against the music coming from the jukebox. "People like their privacy. Some people like it a whole lot. A guy could get hurt saying things

A Quiet Place to Die

about those people in the wrong places. Or to the wrong people." He spoke the words slowly and carefully, as if to a child, or an idiot.

"Some people travel a long way to make sure their private business stays private. Because people like Rafe Gonzales or Gill Barnett would never understand. And a guy who makes a living fishing in this area doesn't have a lot of options for new employment. Am I making myself perfectly clear, James Willoughby Davis?" The hands on my shoulders tightened.

"Which of you explained that to Lee Aleada?" I asked, ignoring the hands on my shoulders.

Hartley picked up the cards and dropped them onto the wallet, sliding it forward to sit next to my beer. The beer he took and slowly poured into the sink.

"I think we're done here, Mr. Davis," he said. "Keep your nose in your own business, and we won't be pulling your body out of the water at Russian Cove. Johnny Mac is off limits. To Lee Aleada, to you, and to any other nosy busybodies who don't know what's good for them.

He turned his back to me, and walked away from my end of the bar. The hands on my shoulders tightened even more, and I was lifted out of my seat and aimed towards the door.

As I walked out under my own power, I looked over at the dancer on the stage. A petite man, with petite shoes, about the size of the footprints at Pelican Point. I walked out into the darkening late afternoon, and got into my car. I felt for my gun, and smiled. I didn't even have a fat lip.

Driving back to Russian Cove gave me plenty of time to think. Hack Hartley had all but said that outing Johnny Mac was a capital offense. Had Lee Aleada threatened to tell Rafe and Gill about Johnny's orientation? Or had Gill found out, and someone in dainty shoes arranged to meet him at Pelican Point? There had been no signs of struggle, but maybe one surprise push had been enough.

The sun had set by the time I got back to the lodge. I pulled my car into the far corner of the lot, this time for no other reason than that it was the only spot available. The party had obviously started.

I went back to my room to put away the gun, camera, and laptop computer. Then I followed the music to the bar. Unlike other nights, there was a table in front of the door, and a young woman I did not know was selling tickets.

"Five dollar cover," she said as I approached. "But you get a free Vampire, which is normally five bucks, so it's worth it."

"What's a Vampire?" I asked, expecting a smart alec answer.

"Vodka, Chambord, cranberry juice, and a piece of dry ice to make it fog up. You drink it with a straw," she explained. I paid the five dollars and got a ticket.

The place was crowded and noisy, more so than usual, if that was possible. Penny Davis was singing and dancing, and seemed to have forgotten whatever had caused the band to cancel the night before. The show must go on. I fought my way through the room, looking for anyone I knew.

Randy Hanson and Rafe Gonzales were in the usual place right next to the stage, enjoying the view as the singer belled out her skirt with each spin. I semaphored a hello, and went to look for Valerie.

Abigail McDougal had deputized Maria and someone I didn't know to help behind the bar, and they still weren't keeping up. Maria was chipping dry ice from deep in the freezer built into the bar, and dropping pieces into an assembly line of blood-red drinks supplied by the other women. A thin straw completed the drink, and Abigail exchanged drinks for tickets as fast as she could.

I lifted the bar gate and slipped through the door to the stairs, and went up to the office, where I knocked on the locked door.

It opened as I was preparing to knock again. I slipped inside and closed the door against the noise from below.

A Quiet Place to Die

"How was bar hopping?" Valerie asked.

"Confusing. It seems like I now have three suspects for each murder. Every time I try to narrow it down, someone gives me a reason to add them to the suspect list." I sat down on the computer desk, one leg on the floor.

"I found your girl," Valerie said.

"Sarah? The four-year-old?"

"Sarah Colter. Or at least her mother, Daphne Colter. About four and a half years ago, McDougal started paying hospital bills for Daphne. Obstetrics. Big bill on September 29." Valerie said.

"Her birthday. Do we have an address?" I asked.

"Point Arena," Valerie said, looking to the computer to get a street and number.

"Should be easy to find," I said. "That place has what, five people living there?"

"You're such a city snob," Valerie said.

"I just drove by there twice today. Oh, this is Point Arena, wasn't it?"

"Jimmy! It's a charming little town. Don't be such a pill. What did you find out today?"

"Hack Hartley, no relation to Dave Hartley, as much as threatened my life if I mentioned that Johnny Mac wasn't straight as a sunbeam. And definitely implied that Lee Aleada got what he deserved for messing in that direction."

"So he's a suspect in Lee's murder," Valerie said.

"Someone at the bar might also be suspect in Gill Barnett's murder. Barnett might have found out, and there's a cross-dressing dancer at the bar wearing shoes that would fit the prints at Pelican Point.

I got the feeling Gill Barnett was not well liked in that community."
I stood up and tried to pace in the small room.

"Danny McDougal goes to his illegitimate daughter's fourth
birthday party. He's drunk. He pulls over, scraping the guardrail,
and then something happens. He smothers himself and someone
makes it look like an accident? Rafe comes along and smothers the
drunk guy?" I turned and paced back to the desk.

"Then Lee Aleada comes to find out. He pisses off Hack Hartley
and gets killed with McDougal's gun? How does Hack know about
the gun? So maybe Aleada pisses off Johnny Mac? Or maybe he
finds out Rafe killed Danny and so Rafe has to shut him up?" I sat
down on the desk again.

"Then there's Gill Barnett. Family man. Takes his kids to school
every day. Has an affair with the pretty singer. Takes the family
car out to Pelican Point, where someone in fancy shoes pushes him
off the cliff. The jilted lover? The cross-dresser? The wife who
found out about the affair?"

Valerie had been patient. She had watched me struggle to put a
case together before. She brought up another point. "Are the three
murders related? If Rafe killed Aleada because he had tied him to
McDougal, then McDougal and Aleada are related. If Aleada died
to protect Johnny's secret, maybe they aren't related. If Gill died to
protect Johnny, same deal. If Gill died because of some affair, same
deal. But you told me once before, murders committed close in
time are always related. Murderers are rare."

"So how does Gill Barnett fit into McDougal's and Aleada's
murders? I'll be damned if I can make that fit." I stood up again,
exasperated.

"I'm going downstairs to talk to a pretty lady," I said. "Another
pretty lady, I mean," I said, bowing to Valerie.

"You're such a charmer," she said, sarcastically.

I opened the door and the flood of noise attacked me. We locked
up, and walked down the stairs.

The crowd was as noisy as ever. Quite a few were in costume. None were naked, although a few came close. We squeezed our way up to the stage, where Rafe and Randy were still sitting, beer glasses empty, Rafe clapping in time to the music. Valerie began to dance, more of a wiggle in the crowded space available.

Communication impossible, we milled around through four more songs before, mercifully, the band declared a break. I fought through the crowd to meet Penny Dixon at the bar. I waited while she drained her glass of water, and then I handed her my business card.

"I love your band," I shouted. "I'm a reporter. I would love to interview you for a piece I'm writing. For the Chronicle."

The singer held the card up to read it. She seemed flattered, which was my intention. But her face screwed up after she had a moment to think. "Now?" she asked.

"Tomorrow," I said as loudly as I could. "Is there a time that is good for you?"

She looked at the card again. "I'll call you," she shouted, nodding enthusiastically. She turned away, and made for the stage again. I worked my way back to Valerie.

"I have an interview with the lady," I said. "Tomorrow."

"Good boy!" she shouted. The band started up again. I tried to shout to her, but she could not hear me. I pulled out my phone, and nearly lost it as someone bumped my arm. I opened it and texted to her. "I'm going to bed." I handed her the phone to read. She began typing. "Party pooper." She handed the phone back to me. I closed the phone and put it back into my pocket, then started backing away, and Valerie waved goodbye.

Outside the door, the noise miraculously diminished by four inches of heavy planking, the woman at the table smiled.

"How did you like the Vampire?" she said.

I searched in my pocket and found the ticket. "I guess I forgot to get mine," I said. "Here, have one on me." I handed the ticket to her.

"I don't know if I can give you a refund," the woman said. "We've never done tickets before."

"It seems to make things go faster at the bar," I said. "Nobody has to make change."

"That new bookkeeper came up with it. She told Abby she had to advertise, and hire more people, and she came up with the ticket thing so everyone inside at least paid something, no freeloaders."

"So you're a new hire?" I asked.

"No, I usually just help Maria on weekends. But this is great, I get work in the middle of the week, and it's easy work, too."

A couple came up to the ticket table, and I waved goodbye to the woman at the table. A blast of noise chased me towards my room as the couple entered the bar.

Once in my room, the noisy bar a distant memory, I sank into the chair in front of the laptop computer. I was tired. I began typing in my report on the day's activities, and what I had learned or suspected. The abridged version went to Corcoran and Silvia. I followed up with the extra details to Silvia alone, including the news about Daphne Colter.

Business done, I surfed to TinyDancer1221's blog. It had been updated with a touching eulogy for Starfish. One line in particular had me sitting up straight, no longer weary from the long day.

"He said he would never go back to prison. I guess he was right."

Gill Barnett was an ex-con? Why hadn't that been in Aleada's notes? I searched through the notes again, in case I had missed it. There was no mention of a criminal record.

I sent off another email, to Corcoran and Silvia, asking for details on the criminal history of Gill Barnett, and letting both of them know that not informing me of this critical piece of information was very bad form.

I closed the laptop, and undressed for bed. Why had he told Penny he would never go back to prison? That is something I would expect someone to say only if they had committed another crime. Or had been asked to commit another crime. Had Rafe asked him to be an accomplice in killing McDougal? Had he been asked to keep quiet about something he knew?

I slid under the covers, my mind wandering into all the corners of the case, trying to fit Gill Barnett into the whole thing. Every time I tried, some part didn't fit. And why had Randy Hanson led me north, to two little towns that had no bikers, let alone biker bars?

I had been right to retire after being shot. I was no good at this anymore.

The dreams I had that night included pretty women with guns, bikers with dainty shoes, and vampires drinking from cocktail glasses. None of it helped me solve anything.

§

Daphne Colter

Blue jays at my window. What did they find so fascinating there?

I got out of bed, and went straight to the shower. I was there a long time. No brilliant answers came to me. I dressed, and was ready to go down to breakfast and still no knock from Valerie's room.

I opened the door to her room, expecting to find the second door shut. Instead, I was looking into her room. She was sprawled across the bed, still dressed, snoring softly. I closed the door quietly, and left my room, walking down to the breakfast room.

Randy Hanson was already there, somehow having beaten Gina and George to breakfast.

"Good morning," I said, noticing he already had coffee. It actually smelled good.

"Some party last night, eh?" he said. He slurped noisily at the coffee. I noticed it was black.

"I'm afraid I missed the last half of it," I said. "Had to get some notes written down. Did you know Gill Barnett was an ex-con?"

He raised his eyebrows and shook his head. "Does that make him a suspect?"

"Not by itself," I said. "But when added to him lying about his whereabouts the night McDougal died, it doesn't help. Not that those two things add up to squat. And I can't think of why it would make someone push him off a cliff. It just seems like an important piece of evidence, and I hate it when important pieces of evidence don't help anything make sense."

Hanson thought about that, slurping noisily at his coffee again. "Maybe he was an accomplice to one of the murders, and the other guy didn't want a witness hanging around."

A Quiet Place to Die

I'd thought of that. "That might explain the lack of a struggle at the cliff. He wasn't expecting his buddy to shove him off. But if he were helping Rafe Gonzales kill McDougal, we'd have seen Rafe's footprints, not some woman's. If he'd helped someone kill Lee Aleada, again, we'd expect larger prints. It leads to a small woman's involvement in one or both of the first murders, and I can't make motive and opportunity that way."

The door to the kitchen opened, and the woman from the ticket table entered, carrying a carafe of coffee and several cups and saucers.

"Good morning! I remember you," she said, placing a cup down in front of me. She poured wonderful smelling coffee into the cup.

"Where's Abigail?" I asked.

"Sleeping in. Like she used to when Danny was running the place. We made a killing last night. I think some of us will be going full-time if she can keep it up."

I took a sip of the coffee. It was wonderful. "Where did the coffee come from?" I asked.

"There's a really neat machine in the bar. Makes all kinds of coffee, just like at Starbucks," she said, carrying the empty tray back to the kitchen door. "You want breakfast, or do you want to wait for more guests?"

"We'll wait," Randy said, watching her disappear through the door.

I tried to find a polite way of asking Randy why he lied to me. It took me a few mental tries. "So, when was the last time you saw any bikers from Caspar around here?" I asked.

He didn't hesitate. "The day Aleada got shot. Two of them were here. Big muscular guys in leathers. Fancy bikes, too."

"What made you think they were from Caspar and Pine Grove?" I pressed on.

"They said they were. They were talking to Johnny Mac. I came up to say hello, who are your friends, and they said they weren't friends; they were just passing through from up north. I said up north like Caspar or Pine Grove? They said yeah, both of them, and then they got pissed off about something and told me to buzz off and mind my own business. Just wham, total mood swing. I figured they were on meth or something, and I got out of there."

I took another sip of coffee, inhaling deeply. "Did Johnny Mac leave too?"

"No," Hanson said, putting down his cup. "He kept talking to them after they got nasty. He doesn't scare easily, not like us old farts. When I heard the choppers start up as they were leaving, I went over to where I could see the parking lot, and Johnny Mac was there, watching them leave."

"So they could have been from anywhere, and just said they were from up north," I said.

"I guess so," Hanson said, not seeing why it might be important. I pulled out my phone, and scrolled through Aleada's notes until I found candid shots from his cell phone. It is easy to get photos when you're pretending to be on a phone call, if you turn off the flash. The pictures turn out a little blurry sometimes, but that's why you take a lot of them.

"Could the bikers have been these two guys?" I asked, flipping between the two photos.

"That guy, definitely," Hanson said. "The one with that little soul patch thing. The other guy maybe, he wasn't talking, so I didn't pay much attention to him."

Dave Hartley and Janet came in. Dave had the laptop.

"Hey there!" he called to me. "We got a lot of the names. Almost all of them." He sat down, opened the laptop, and waited for it to boot up. Janet poured coffee for both of them.

A Quiet Place to Die

"I made a slideshow by cropping the faces into new pictures and labeling them with the names. This is so cool, check it out." He turned the laptop around, and a Valerie's face was fading out, being replaced by Gina's. Below the face were the words Gina Franco.

"That is very cool," I said, humoring Hartley. "Can you email that to me?" I pulled out my business card and pointed to the email address.

The door to the kitchen opened again. "That's a little better," the ticket table woman said, bringing in another carafe of coffee. She picked up the first one, sloshed the remaining coffee in it to see how much remained, and then topped up cups until it was empty.

"You about ready for breakfast?" she asked. Dave answered enthusiastically in the affirmative, still entering something on the keyboard.

"What's your name, honey?" Hanson asked.

"I'm Jill," she said. "Jill Tarrington." She disappeared through the kitchen door again.

Valerie came in, followed by Gina and George.

"Coffee," Valerie said, imitating a zombie movie. She sat down with a thump and reached for the carafe.

"These two closed down the party last night," George said. "They really loved that fog drink. I must have gone out for more tickets a dozen times."

Gina said nothing, eyeing the coffee carafe. When Valerie put it down, she grabbed it like a lifeline.

Breakfast was great. Valerie and Gina just drank coffee.

After breakfast, I went back to my room to check my email. Hartley's slide show was there, and I saved that to the disk for later. The one I was looking for was the one from Corcoran. It said nothing, but had an attachment. It was the public record of one

William Gilbert Barnett. Three years in Corcoran State Prison for attempted murder. I wondered if the deputy realized there was a prison named for him.

If Aleada had been searching for Gill Barnett, he wouldn't have found the record I was reading. That may be why Barnett decided to use his middle name. I searched the web for old newspaper stories about William Gilbert Barnett, but they were sketchy. Some bar fight involving a bottle. His public defender cut a deal with the prosecutor. A man who could have afforded an attorney would probably have gotten probation at most.

Corcoran State was hard time. Juan Corona, Charles Manson, Sirhan Sirhan, they were all there, although not in the general population. If you didn't have a gang affiliation before you got there, and you couldn't pay for protection, life would be difficult. For a nineteen-year-old, it must have been hell.

My cell phone rang. I answered with a hello. "Is this Jimmy Davis, freelance journalist?" said Penny Dixon's voice. The voice was rough from singing the night before.

"This must be the amazing Penelope Dixon," I said, diving straight into flattery.

"You still want to do an article about the band?" she asked.

"Absolutely. Is there a time and place that works best for you? Where are you?" I asked.

"I live in Mendocino. You want me to come down there, or do you want to come up here?"

I was eager to keep her on the hook. "I'll come to you," I said. "Is there a nice quiet place we can do the interview? A restaurant or something? I'll be bringing a recorder."

"There's Rosie's," she said, "It's pretty dead on a Friday afternoon. How about five o'clock?"

"Perfect," I said. "I hear they have good pie there. My treat."

"Ok, then," she said. "Rosie's at five. Anything else?"

"That's it. See you at five." We said goodbyes, and I closed the phone.

I thought about what I was going to ask her. Kill anyone lately? How many? Three? Oh, dear, you'll be wanting more pie then, that must work up an appetite.

I heard Valerie enter her room. A minute or so later, she opened the door between the rooms, and walked into mine.

"I feel so awful," she said. "Aspirin isn't helping." She flopped down on my unmade bed.

"How's the accounting going?" I asked. "Seems like you made a few suggestions on how to run the business better."

"That worked out pretty well, didn't it? You know how hard it is to find a roll of tickets around here? I had to beg some from a school up in Fort Bragg." She sat up, and then flopped down again, her arms slapping the mattress loudly.

"So, what are your plans for the day?" I asked.

"I'm just going to curl up and die," she said.

"After that, I mean."

"I have the books all straight. Next, I'm going to make up a how-to book for the business. When this bill comes in, do this, when this invoice comes in, do that. A cookbook for running a lodge. She needs to advertise. The salmon ban is killing this place, but there are diving magazines where she could advertise special abalone weekends and there's still lingcod fishing, and other things. That huge empty lot on the south side is part of the property, and I told her she should make it a campground; charge some really low rate for tents, like five bucks a night. Then have rainy day specials, where the receipt for the campground gets you a room for half price. There are all kinds of things she should be doing."

"If she's not in jail for murder or insurance fraud," I said.

"I don't think she did anything," Valerie said, still flat on her back. "She's like some high-functioning autistic. She relates to people funny. She just does her job, and doesn't mingle much, doesn't say much, doesn't get jokes. She doesn't plan far enough ahead to do bad things."

I looked over at her. She had her eyes closed, and she was rocking her head left to right. "Those are the kind to watch," I said. "The kind of people you can't understand. You don't know what their motivations are, or how they think. They're unpredictable. She might be impulsive."

She opened one eye. "Look who's talking. Some guy with a hung over floozy in his bed."

I let that comment alone. I walked over to my suitcase and took out the shoulder holster again, and put it on.

"Where are you going that you need a gun?" Valerie asked, sitting up, if a bit wobbly.

"I'm going to call on Daphne Colter."

"And you need a gun for that?" she asked.

"Lee Aleada knew that sometimes you have to be a target to get people to come to you. He just wasn't careful enough. I'm careful." I adjusted the gun, and put on the thin jacket to hide it. "Besides, she just might be pretty, and I've been warned about those types."

Valerie got up off the bed, a bit unsteady. "I need another shower," she said, and walked into her room. She didn't shut the door.

"Have fun," I called. "I'll be in Point Arena."

I walked down the stairs to the parking lot, and got into my car. I set the laptop computer on the passenger seat, and then entered the address into the GPS. I set it to record the trip, and drove onto the highway.

Daphne Colter did not have a listed number. She may be one of the many these days that only used a cell phone. But I had her address, and I would just walk up and knock on the door, and maybe apologize for not calling first. Of course, it was likely that she would be at work during the day, and all I would get out of the trip would be photos, and maybe some canvassing of the neighbors.

Two motorcycles passed me, heading south. They were going at high speed, and I couldn't tell if the riders were anyone I knew. But they wore sleeveless leather vests; I could see that from behind. Where had Johnny Mac been last night? Why wasn't he up near the stage with Rafe and Randy?

When I turned off the highway, I revised my opinion about Point Arena. Driving through, I estimated it might hold as many as 500 people. There were yard signs for local elections, and a poster advertizing the Point Arena Centennial Year. I drove past a theater, shops, restaurants, a yoga studio, a dental center. There were signs for a zebra preserve. Valerie was going to love this place. Still a little small for me, though.

The GPS announced that I had arrived at my destination. It was off by a couple of blocks, but I was used to that in rural areas. I found Daphne Colter's house. I got out the camera, and snapped a few photos of the neighborhood, and the house. I got out of the car and walked around to the front of the house. A four-year-old was playing in a sandbox. I backed away, and went back to the car.

I hadn't really expected anyone to be home. It could be a babysitter. Or it could be Daphne herself. I thought through how I would handle each situation.

I went to the rear of the Camry and opened the trunk. The gift-wrapped box was there, and I picked it up and shut the trunk again. Walking back to the house, I smiled at the little girl, and walked up to the door. The door itself was open, so whoever was inside could hear the child playing through the screen door. I rang the bell.

The woman who came to the door was probably in her mid forties. She was wiping her hands on a dishtowel. "Can I help you?" she asked.

"I'm looking for Daphne Colter," I said. "I'm a journalist. I'm doing a piece about Daniel McDougal, and I am hoping I can take a moment of your time to talk for a bit?"

She looked down at the package in my hands. "What's in the box?"

"Something Danny wanted Sarah to have," I said. Her curiosity was piqued. She invited me in.

"Who've you been talking to?" she asked. The house was small, the kitchen was at one side of the front room, and there was an open door leading to a single bedroom. Toys were scattered about both rooms. She sat down on a worn couch, and I sat down at the other end. I placed the box between us.

"It's a teddy bear," I said. "He had one like it in the car when he died, on his way here. That one is still in the sheriff's evidence locker, so I brought its twin. It seemed like the right thing to do, I'm sorry if I was being presumptuous..."

"Murdered, you mean. When he was murdered." She picked up the box, running her hands over the ribbon. Tears welled up in her eyes. I looked down at the box.

"Mrs. Colter," I said. "Do you know who killed Danny McDougal?"

"Miss," she said. "And damn right I know. I told that deputy it was Abby, but he wouldn't listen to me. He didn't believe Danny was Sarah's father. And she cremated him so I can't prove it."

I hesitated, thinking through how I could ask delicately. "Can you help me prove that he was murdered?"

Tears fell down her cheeks, and she wiped at her face. More tears fell. She closed her eyes. "He told me he was going to change his will, so when he died I would get the property. That bitch killed her own father, to make sure she got it all." More tears fell silently. I waited before continuing.

"Had he talked to anyone professionally about changing the will? A lawyer perhaps? A notary?" I spoke quietly, keeping my tone gentle and conspiratorial.

She shrugged her shoulders. "I don't know. He was old, you know, and drank hard, smoked a lot, he didn't have any dreams of living to a hundred or anything. He knew he didn't have a lot of time, but he thought he'd have enough. He must have told her, though. That's why she did it. Killed my Danny." She closed her eyes again, and wiped the tears with her dishtowel.

"Do you have any letters from Danny? Anything written down?"

"From Danny? He never wrote anything. Nobody writes letters anymore. Everybody has a cell phone. But he never called. He'd just show up, either here or at the café when I was at work."

It was difficult to keep from badgering the woman. This was going to take time. "So there were people at work who knew about you and Danny?"

"Oh, God no. Danny was really careful. He never wanted anybody to know about us. It's a sin, you know, and he was very Catholic, very old-fashioned. I have one photograph, just one, of him holding Sarah." She got up from the couch, and walked into the bedroom. The bed was neatly made, I could see from the couch. Toys were all over the place, but the bed was made. I looked into the kitchen. From my seat on the couch, I could not see into the sink, but there were no dirty dishes in evidence. The house was clean and neat, except for the toys.

Daphne came out of the bedroom holding an unframed photograph of Danny McDougal holding a baby, perhaps a year old.

"Can I take a photo of this?" I said, pulling my phone out of my pocket.

"Have at it," she said, handing me the photograph. I placed it on the couch, and framed it in the screen on the phone and pressed the shutter release. The phone flashed. I used the zoom to make sure the focus was OK, and then handed the picture back to Daphne.

"What can you tell me about the relationship between Abigail and Danny McDougal?" I asked.

"I only saw her once. Danny didn't want me to ever go up there. But he'd tell me about fights they had. She didn't like him drinking. His wife died in a car wreck because she was drinking. You know Abby doesn't drink? She tends the damn bar and hands out the stuff, but she won't touch a drop. Hypocrite."

"What kind of fights?" I asked.

"She's not normal, you know? They had to send her to special schools, like for dumb kids. She's smart, but she has problems. Problems with people. She couldn't understand Danny. She couldn't understand normal people. They'd have fights and he wouldn't know what was making her mad. Like he'd put something in the wrong place and she'd fly off the handle. That's usually when he'd show up here."

Sarah came in. Daphne jumped up and hurried over to catch her.

"You have sand all over your shoes and in your pants cuffs, honey. Come out on the porch and we'll stomp it off, Ok? Here, let's roll down your pants and brush off all the sand."

Sarah stomped loudly on the porch, laughing and jumping. Once thoroughly dusted off, the two came back into the house. Daphne grabbed a broom and swept off the sand from the floor, and then from the porch.

Sarah was staring at the gift-wrapped box. Daphne put the broom away, and sat back down on the couch. "Who got a present?" Sarah asked.

Daphne looked up at me, then at the box, then at Sarah. "You did, honey." She handed the box to her.

"I already had my birthday," she said to me. She began carefully peeling the bow from the package, making sure she didn't tear the paper. "We had a party, mommy and me. We had a cake and candles, and I made a wish but I can't tell anybody or it won't come true. Danny said he would bring a surprise but he didn't come."

She found the tape holding the ribbon, and peeled it off the package. "This is from Danny," I said. "This is the surprise he wanted to bring you." She undid the tape from the wrapping paper and then folded it neatly and put it next to the bow and ribbon. I had never seen someone this young do anything other than rip a present open. But to Sarah, the packaging seemed as important as the contents.

She looked up at her mother, eyes sparkling. The unwrapped box sat in front of her, the lid still on. "Are you ready?" she said, a big grin on her face, watching her mother intently.

"I'm ready," Daphne said, pretending to be excited by the impending unveiling. She leaned forward. Sarah raised the lid over her head and looked inside the box.

"It's the one in the window! He remembered! Look it has the ribbon and the little book, and the sparkly collar!" She picked up the bear and hugged it to her chest. She stood up awkwardly, and rushed over to Daphne for a group hug. Daphne wiped at tears again, but more came.

"We're going to have a party," Sarah said to her mother. "It's his birthday, you know." She jumped up and ran into the bedroom with the bear, and began setting up toy plates and glasses for the party.

Daphne wiped her face again, and reached to place the wrapping paper and bow into the box. "That was very nice of you," she said.

"The least I could do," I almost whispered. I cleared my throat. "You know, I've spent the last four days at the lodge. Abigail seems pretty well adjusted. She's running the place herself now. Maybe the picture Danny painted for you might be, well, a little overstated?"

She considered this. "She's smart. But those people can be smart and still not be right, not be normal. She has routines; Danny said those were really important to her. As long as she can do things the same way each day, she's Ok, but as soon as something changes, she needs someone else to tell her what to do, set up a new routine. Then she's back on track. But when things aren't going like she planned, who knows what she'd do. She gets out of control. Does weird things."

Sarah, in the bedroom, was urging the bear to blow out the candles on his imaginary birthday cake. "What kind of weird things?" I asked.

"She collects road kill. She brings them home and buries them somewhere, with little wooden crosses, all neat in rows, with flowers growing on the graves. She feeds the raccoons at the lodge, and one day one of them bit Danny on the hand. He got mad, and set up a Havahart trap to catch them so he could let them go up at the state park. But when one got caught, Abby took the trap, set it out in her road kill graveyard, and made it spend the night there. Then in the morning, she let it go again, and hid the trap from Danny. Weird stuff like that. Thinking a raccoon would be scared of a road kill graveyard and not bite people again."

I looked at Daphne as she watched her daughter play. The tears had dried, and she seemed relaxed. "That doesn't sound exactly, well, homicidal, though, does it?" I asked.

"You're starting to sound like that deputy," she said.

"Corcoran?"

"That's him. Smug shit, he didn't even investigate until that insurance guy came around. He made it sound like *I* was the one who was nuts." She looked down at her feet.

"You're not nuts," I said. "You're being very helpful. Did you speak to Lee Aleada?"

"Who?"

"The insurance investigator. His name was Lee Aleada," I prompted.

"He never came around. I read about him getting killed in the newspaper. They said the deputy started investigating after the insurance company smelled something rotten. But I already told him she killed Danny. And he didn't do anything. I vote you know, and I'm sure not voting for that idiot." She threw her dishtowel in the general direction of the sink. I thought that seemed uncharacteristic for someone who kept a neat house and taught her daughter to carefully save wrapping paper.

I stood up, and got a card out of my wallet. "If there is anything else you remember, or think I should know, you can reach me here," I said, handing her the card.

"You just going to write about it, and that's it?" she said, reading the card.

"Sometimes writing about something is the best way to get people's attention," I said. "Justice sometimes happens faster when people know the world is paying attention."

She walked with me to the door, and held the screen door open for me. "Thank you again for your help," I said.

She looked back into the bedroom where Sarah was playing with the teddy bear. "Thank you. I know you didn't have to do that."

"Like I said," I repeated, "it's the least I could do. Give me a call, even if it's just to touch base." I walked down the steps of the porch and onto the sidewalk. She watched until I turned the corner.

I reached into my pocket for the pen recorder that had been dutifully logging the entire conversation, and I turned it off. I would need to go over the conversation again, when it wasn't personal, when I wasn't emotionally involved.

The drive back to Russian Cove did not register in my conscious mind. I was going over what I had learned today, and was driving on autopilot.

Did Abigail McDougal kill her father? This morning I would have considered the idea farfetched. I may have considered it before and discarded it easily. Was she mentally unstable? She was not good at small talk, but does that make someone homicidal? Someone who loved raccoons, and buried their unfortunate relatives under flowers?

As I neared Russian Cove, two motorcycles roared past me, going south at perhaps ninety miles an hour, far too fast for the winding highway. The sudden attack of sound caused me to jerk out of my reverie so quickly I almost swerved off the road. I felt for my gun as I checked the rear view mirror, but they were gone around a bend. I felt foolish, but my heart was racing. I should pay more attention to the road.

It was getting close to three thirty, and it made no sense to stop at the lodge if I had to be in Mendocino at five. I'd get there early, and maybe eat some pie at Rosie's while I waited. I could check my email on the laptop.

It didn't take long to find Rosie's Café. Mendocino may be the second largest town on this part of the coast, but it still isn't that big. There were only two other customers, but the place seemed crowded due to all the small tables wedged into every square yard of the small café. I picked a table near a wall socket for the laptop, but also where I'd be facing the door, and could look out the window into the parking lot. Wearing a gun always made me want to keep my back to a wall.

I ordered a Marionberry pie alamode and a glass of milk at the counter, and went to my table to set up the computer. There was an email from Silvia. She had found the birth records for Sarah Colter. I wondered whether she had found them before or after I emailed her with Valerie's discovery of the same information. Not that I cared how much extra work I had caused Silvia.

My slice of pie arrived, and I now understood Corcoran's weight problem. It was a quarter of a pie, heated nearly to incandescence, and then smothered with two huge scoops of vanilla ice cream. I wouldn't need to eat for the rest of the day. Maybe the whole week.

Nevertheless, I had finished the pie and was scraping the last molecules of ice cream from the plate when a Mazda Miata entered the parking lot. The top was down, and a petite redhead with her hair held back in a ponytail stepped out. I reached into my pocket and turned on the pen recorder. But I also set the laptop to record video, and positioned the camera to face the seat opposite me.

I waved as she came in. She smiled and went to the counter to order a coffee. Then she came to sit down across from me.

"Is it all right with you if I record this?" I said, pointing to the small video image of Penny in the laptop display. "It makes it so much easier than taking notes. This way we can just chat," I said.

"That's kind of neat," she said, making faces at the camera. "I've never done this, do you, like, have a list of questions or something?"

"I usually just wing it," I said. "I like to be informal and friendly. Can we start with when the band got together?"

She nodded, and launched into the story, most of which I already knew from reading the web site and the private blog. As she spoke, her eyes found it hard to decide whether to look at me, or the image of herself on the laptop screen. She enjoyed watching herself, even in a tiny little window.

I asked a good half hour of questions about the band. Who wrote the songs, was a recording coming out, what venues are coming up, where do you want to take the music in the future? She became comfortable with me asking questions.

"Do you have any favorite fans?" I asked. She hesitated.

"They're all special," she finally said. "Some of the rowdier guys in the front row more than others, maybe." The corners of her eyes creased a little as she smiled. She knew I sat with Rafe and Johnny Mac in the front row. She also knew that I was the one who had found Gill Barnett's body.

"You recently cancelled an appearance. What happened?" I asked.

She looked at herself in the laptop screen again. She was performing for the camera. She wasn't talking to me, so it was Ok that we both knew the answer to the question. She was speaking to her audience.

"One of our special fans died," she said. There was no catch in her voice as she spoke. "Gill Barnett. They found his body that day, in the water. It was really sad. It just didn't feel right to us to play happy music that night. He was such a sweet guy." Here she showed some emotion. I couldn't tell if she was acting.

"Does anyone know what happened that night at Pelican Point?" I asked.

She shook her head. "I don't think so. The funeral is Sunday. I got invited."

This was news. I was unaware of any funeral plans, but I wouldn't have been notified. But why would Penny Dixon have been invited? And why did she want me to know that she had?

"So you were a friend of the family?" I said after I had collected my thoughts.

"I knew Gill and Catherine," she said. "And the kids. Those poor kids. His family was very important to Gill." She watched herself in the video. Practicing for the funeral?

I reached over and switched off the video recording program, and closed the lid on the laptop. I did not shut off the pen recorder.

"Did Gill have any enemies?" I asked. "Maybe someone from his past or someone he may have met in prison?"

A Quiet Place to Die

She looked up at me in dismay. "No one is supposed to know about that. Are you going to print that? The kids don't know he was in prison. You can't print that!"

I placed my hand on hers, across the table. "None of what we say now is for publication," I said. "That's why we're not recording. It's just that I was the one who found him, and I'm trying to get to know the guy, get some idea of what his life was like. It's hard finding a body like that. You want to know. Am I making sense?" I said, trying to elicit compassion, to keep her talking.

"Everyone loved Gill," she said, calming down. "He was really sweet, a really sweet guy."

"When was the last time you saw Gill?" I asked.

She looked at me, studying my expression. I tried to think about bunny rabbits and kittens, to keep a poker face.

"He was at McDougal's Sunday night," she said. "In the front row with Rafe and Johnny Mac. He likes to sing along with the bawdy ballads. Shouts out the naughty bits. Shouted. He used to."

"You didn't see him Monday night?" I asked.

"He wasn't with them that night," she said. She picked up her empty coffee cup and tried to sip the last cold drop, and then put it down.

"Do you think what happened to Gill is related in any way to the other two murders?" I asked.

She looked up quickly and studied my face again. "You mean that insurance guy? Danny had a heart attack; Gill didn't have anything to do with that." She continued looking straight at me, as if I were a strange dog in her yard.

"Who do you think killed the insurance investigator?" I asked.

"That guy? He was pissing everybody off. He made it sound like everybody in the world was a killer, and had it in for Danny. He didn't make any friends at all; he was telling everybody that their friends could be murderers. But I don't think it was anybody around here that killed him. People like that probably have enemies all over the place, who follow them around. There were lots of strangers around that night. McDougal's was packed. Everybody was curious about the wake."

This was more news. "How so?" I asked, keeping the question wide open. Penny seemed relieved that the conversation was going in a different direction now.

"Abigail made it a big deal. Danny had written down a big list of what he wanted at his wake. He like made up this list when his wife died a bunch of years ago, and Abigail kept it. She insisted on doing everything exactly like it said on the list. The songs on the stereo, the exact number of people, no extras, the brands of whiskey, it went on and on. Everything had to be just so. And she never cried. She got mad sometimes, if something wasn't right, and she got it fixed, but she never cried. That was Wednesday, the first day of October. She has this thing about October; it's like a really special month or something." She tried to take another sip from her empty coffee cup. She looked over at the counter as if she were going to order a refill, but decided against it.

She continued. "So that was Wednesday. Friday nights are usually big at McDougal's, especially in October, when they do beer things, you know like in Germany, but the Friday after the wake there was nothing, the bar was closed. So the next week, when the bar is open again, that Friday night was packed, because everybody had heard about the weird wake and everybody was curious. And then that guy gets shot down at the cove. Nobody found the guy until the next morning; nobody heard anything because everybody was in the bar."

"Everyone except for Lee Aleada," I said.

"That's why I said it was probably some stranger," Penny said. "All the locals were at the bar."

"But the bar closes fairly early, for a bar I mean, at least since Danny died, isn't that right?" I asked.

"It's been getting earlier. Abby used to keep the bar open until two in the morning, but since she had to do the breakfast thing it was about eleven or so that night, and she closes even earlier now."

I looked at Penny, trying to be casual. "But Aleada was shot sometime after midnight," I said.

"Oh," Penny said simply. She looked like this had actually not occurred to her. "Wow. So it could be someone we know."

I looked at my watch. "You're on in about an hour. Do you need to get ready or something?"

"Oh, wow, yes. I need to take a shower and get dressed." She stood up.

"This is going to be a great article on the band," I said, pointing to the laptop. "Some great stuff in there."

She smiled, genuinely happy, and perhaps relieved it was all over. I stood and collected the laptop and charger, and she held the door for me as we left the café. I was arranging the laptop on the seat when the Miata roared to life, and she was off down the road.

I reached into my jacket past my gun and shut off the pen recorder. This was a conversation I would have to go over a few times before I could pick out all the nuance. She was a born performer.

§

Raphael Gonzales

The sun was low when I got back to Russian Cove. I parked at the end of the lot, now partly just out of habit, and walked up to my room. It felt good to remove the shoulder holster and tuck it away in my suitcase. I set up the laptop on the desk and let it charge some more. You never know when a full battery will be needed.

I left my room and walked over to the reception desk. Jill Tarrington was there, rubbing spray wax into the big wooden counter.

"Hey there," she said. "I still owe you a drink from last night."

There were a couple of ways I could take that statement. I decided not to resolve the ambiguity by remaining ambiguous myself. I checked my watch.

"A little early for me," I said. "How about I catch you later?" I smiled and continued past her up to the big doors to the bar. She smiled back and nodded, going back to her polishing. I pulled the big door open and went into the bar.

Abigail and Maria were setting up large Jack O' Lanterns on the stage, and small ones on each table. There was a large sheet of plastic drop cloth draped over a table, and it was covered in Jack O' Lantern brains. The murder weapons were still arrayed on the table. Long thin knives and big sharp metal spoons.

Some of the pumpkins had carefully symmetrical faces in the traditional triangle motif. Others were more fanciful, with artfully carved eyes and various flavors of nose and grin. I could guess which of the two artists had done each one.

"Is Valerie up in the office?" I called out to the women.

"Si," Maria said, pointing upstairs. Abigail looked up at me, and then went back to arranging the decorations in perfect rows. I walked to the bar, lifted the gate, and went upstairs. The door opened at my knock, and Valerie waved me in.

A Quiet Place to Die

"So, how did it go in Point Arena?" she asked.

"Interesting," I said. "Daphne Colter is sure that Abigail killed her father. She says he was about to change his will, to leave the lodge to Daphne, and Abby found out about it."

Valerie gave me a puzzled look and went to the file cabinet. She pulled open the second drawer, and thumbed through the labeled tabs until she found the folder she wanted, and extracted it.

"I spent most of the afternoon getting these all organized," she said. She pulled out a copy of the instructions for the wake. "I think he wrote this mostly as a joke, and Abby took it seriously, and very literally." She handed it to me, and then took out a copy of the will.

The will was professionally done. I got out my camera and took photos of each page, zooming in after the first shot to make sure the lawyer's name was clear. There was a list of assets, mostly properties in the area, and bank accounts. The list was divided into two parts. Exhibit A included the bank accounts and the lodge itself, and adjoining properties acquired at different dates. Exhibit B included some properties in nearby towns, and several stock and bond funds.

I'm not a lawyer, but I scanned the document as I photographed it. Exhibit A went to Abigail McDougal in its entirety. Exhibit B was to be divided among all living descendants, after all debts and obligations of the estate were settled. The will was dated August 11th of this year.

"It looks like he *did* change the will," I said. "How many living descendants do you think there are?"

"We know about Sarah. And there's Abby. I didn't see anything when I was looking for Sarah that gave me any hint of any others. All these photos on the wall of Abby growing up, they all just have Abby in them."

I looked around the room. "She could have removed photos that showed a brother or a sister," I said, not believing it myself. There were no blank spaces on the wall where a picture had been taken down, and no nail holes to indicate a missing photo.

Valerie was at the computer. "I've been working out how much tax the estate owes on those properties. I have the purchase prices, and the latest property tax figures, but no real estate comps. If the taxes are paid out of the stocks and bonds, and there are no liens against the properties, it looks like Abby gets a little under five million from the A list, and splits about three million from the B list with Sarah."

My appreciation for Danny McDougal just went up. "That's a lot of money," I said.

"He's been buying up land around here for fifty years. Using rental income to buy more. The guy loved acreage." Valerie printed out the list of estimated values and handed it to me.

"If you're getting six and a half million dollars from your father's estate, is it worth killing him to get another million and a half?" I asked. "If you get caught, you get nothing. It just doesn't sound like something Abby would do. They had the occasional fight, but did she really hate her father? Enough to kill him?"

Valerie slowly spun the chair around to face me. "It doesn't sound right to me either," she said.

"Daphne Colter doesn't know about the will. She thinks he didn't get time to change it. She doesn't know she's getting over a million dollars," I said.

"Technically, she isn't getting anything. She's not a descendant. Sarah gets it. Of course, as the mother, she would control it." Valerie twisted back and forth on the swivel of the chair.

"My point was that Abby hasn't told her," I said.

"So you think she *is* trying to keep it all. That doesn't square either. I showed her all the numbers this morning, and she didn't care. All she cared about was making sure everything was running smoothly, that the taxes were paid and the employees were paid. The money that's not involved in the day-to-day running of the lodge didn't interest her at all. It might as well not have been there."

I thought about this for a time. Then I remembered something. "Did I tell you that Gill Barnett was an ex-con?" I asked.

"That's interesting. Does that change anything?" She went back to twisting the chair back and forth.

"You'd think it would, wouldn't you? But I'll be damned if it makes anything clear. Penny was really upset when I mentioned it. She knew, but Barnett's kids don't know, and I suspect it's a secret the family would like to keep. But it would be a really weak motive for murder. It just doesn't help."

"What was it for?" she asked.

"Attempted murder. Sounds ominous, doesn't it? But he hit some guy with a bottle in a bar fight when he was nineteen. Not even old enough to be allowed in the bar. Did three at Corcoran. Nothing since. It just doesn't fit anywhere." I turned and pretended to bang my head on the wall.

"So what else did Penny say?" Valerie was changing the subject.

"It's what she didn't say. She didn't say she was with him the night he died. She didn't lie to me though. She always said truthful statements that left something out. She is definitely hiding things, and has had a lot of time to think about how to do it. She's running some script in her head. She didn't mention she'd been banging Barnett." I leaned back against the wall, wiggling my feet forward.

"So she's hiding an affair. That's normal."

"It's more than that. She doesn't know whether or not I know about it, or will find out about it. So she has this 'plausible deniability' shield. She never lies; she just changes the question when she answers. There's something more than the affair she's hiding."

I stood up, and put my hand on the doorknob. Valerie stood up too, and we went downstairs. The Jack O' Lanterns had little flashlights in them, and bowls of warm water with dry ice, so the fog would spill out of their mouths.

"That's very creative!" Valerie said to Abby.

"McDougal did it for me every year, for my birthday," Abby said. She did not elaborate.

"When is your birthday?" Valerie asked.

"October 29, every year," came Abby's answer. "McDougal's favorite month."

The band had arrived. Penny Dixon walked into the bar, and saw us talking. "Hey Jimmy!" she called out, spinning around so her skirt belled out. "You going to be in the front row tonight?" She winked at me, and glanced at Valerie, as if sizing up the competition. I remembered after a minute that I could be her father.

"So what's on your list for tomorrow?" Valerie asked.

I was not looking forward to tomorrow. "It's time to call on the widow Barnett," I said. "The day before the funeral. That is not going to be fun."

She took my hand. "So think about the fun part of the job. What's your favorite part of doing all this? Besides getting paid. I know you don't do it just for the money."

I waved my hand at the people entering the bar. "Getting to know all these fascinating and wonderful people," I said. "And finding out which of them is a murderer."

People were starting to fill up the bar. The band was tuning up. Rafael Gonzales and Johnny Mac entered, and made straight for the front row table to claim it.

"Hey, Jimmy!" I turned around to see Randy Hanson and Dave Hartley walking in. "I saw those biker dudes again," Hanson said, coming closer. "Talking to Rafe and Johnny Mac."

I waited for them to join Valerie and me standing in the middle of the collection of foggy lanterned tables. "What were they discussing?" I asked.

Hanson shrugged. "I kept my distance. After the last time, I thought I'd just leave them alone." He began walking towards the table Rafe and Johnny Mac had staked out. The rest of us followed.

Rafe kicked a chair out for Valerie, and we all sat down, except for Dave. "Pitchers?" he asked. Hanson and I both reached for our wallets, but Dave waved us off. "You catch the next round," he said, and headed for the bar.

Rafe seemed to make a point out of putting his arm across the back of Johnny Mac's chair, aiming a look at me. "I hear you've met our friends, Gary and Duke," he said. A very clear message to me.

"Big guys, leather, shiny bikes?" I said.

"That's them. We're short, since Gill is gone. They suck at ling cod fishing, but they can pull up crab pots like two guys each," Gonzales took his arm away from the back of Johnny Mac's chair.

"They'll get the hang of fishing," Johnny Mac said. "When the salmon are open again, they'll be ready." He looked at me and smiled. I was seeing hidden meaning everywhere, but maybe it was just a smile. He seemed genuinely happy. So did Rafe. I wondered when Rafe had found out, and how. That he was comfortable with it raised my estimation of the man a couple notches.

"You guys should take out sport fishermen," Valerie said, leaning towards the two men. "Do a package deal with Abby, room, breakfast, fishing boat, seafood dinner. At least until the salmon fishing comes back. She already advertises in California Game & Fish. Or at least she liked the idea when I said she should. You guys know what synergy is?"

Johnny Mac nodded. "Synergy with McDougal's. Everybody wins. We should talk to Abby," he said, turning to Rafe, who nodded.

Dave arrived with the pitchers and went back for mugs. The band started up, and I got out my camera, in keeping with my cover story. Penny Dixon danced for the camera, keeping her eyes on me as she played her pennywhistle. Everyone seemed relaxed and happy, as if no one had murdered anyone, and no one was worried about being caught.

Dave returned with the mugs, and the night got noisier. Dave was counting tickets, so I assumed Jill was at the front door again, making life easier for Abby and Maria at the bar. Valerie was going to have this place raking in cash in the middle of a recession.

When it was clear that conversation had died in the face of the noise, and the night was devolving into drinking and sneaking peeks up Penny's skirt, I stood up and waved a goodbye to the group, smiling my apologies. Valerie put on an exaggerated sad face, but stayed seated, a half-full beer mug in her hand.

I made my way to the door, dodging people and tables. The woman I didn't know who had been helping out at the bar the night before was refilling pumpkins with dry ice. I smiled and waved at her as I passed by.

Outside the door, the sound safely muffled to EPA approved levels, Jill Tarrington looked up at me from her ticket table. "Did I ever get your name?" she asked.

"Jimmy Davis," I said.

"You leaving early again? That could get to be a bad habit," she said, stacking bills neatly in the small metal box.

"I have a lot of those," I said, smiling at her.

"Then I won't worry about you," she said. "People with bad habits and bars go together. But the more money we make, the more likely I can stay on full time, so don't be a stranger."

I waved and went up to my room. The laptop was waiting there for me to file my report. There wasn't anything I wanted to share with Corcoran, so I just listed whom I had talked to. In the second email to Silvia, I told about Daphne Colter's theories, and what Penny Dixon had said, and what she had left out.

I sent the email, and wondered how I was going to approach Catherine Barnett. As the guy who had found her dead husband? As someone who was writing a lighthearted travel piece about the lodge? No, to get her to talk I was going to have to let her know quite a bit of what I had found out. Things about her dead husband that she was not going to want to hear on the day before his funeral. I needed to figure out how to play that without being immediately thrown out. I didn't have a teddy bear to break the ice.

I showered and got into bed. Tomorrow was not going to be easy.

§

Catherine Barnett

I awoke to a kiss on my forehead. "Rise and shine, Sleeping Beauty," Valerie said in a voice altogether too chipper for the pre-dawn hour.

She was dressed and ready to meet the world. Either beer did not affect her like vodka and dry ice, or she had tempered her consumption out of fear of a repeat of yesterday's hangover.

"I might get out of bed if I had a little privacy," I said.

She looked at me and grinned. "Shy boys shouldn't sleep in the buff," she said. I thought she was going to wait me out, but she walked back into her room and shut the door. I made it to the bathroom without the door opening again.

At breakfast, Jill had set out pastries, and the coffee carafe was full and there were cups on the tray. We were the first to arrive, but we had been anticipated. The coffee was hot and wonderful.

"Are you going to keep me one here?" Valerie asked as I bit into a danish. "I've pretty much exhausted the search for incriminating evidence. I'm spending my time turning Abigail into Conrad Hilton."

I took a sip of coffee to lubricate the pastry, and swallowed. "I'm enjoying your company," I said. "I'm sure Silvia can afford another day or two. How about we don't tell her until we actually catch some bad guys. Having another ear to the ground is always useful."

She eyed the pastries, and seemed to struggle with the decision of whether to take one, or to stick with coffee. Coffee won, but the danish were still putting up a good fight.

"I found the cemetery," she said. "Or flower garden. Rows of pansies, all very neat, with little crosses made from tongue depressors. Randy and I were out walking after the band stopped playing. The moon is still almost full, and you can see all the neat little rows."

A Quiet Place to Die

George and Gina came in, and seemed delighted at the pastry tray. Randy Hanson arrived shortly after.

"So," Hanson said, "the biker dudes are going to be fishermen. Doesn't sound like they'd hang around the scene of the crime if they were our guys, does it?"

He sat down, grabbed a pastry at random, and bit off half of it while he poured coffee into a cup.

"Or it could be they're here to see if there were any witnesses they needed to make disappear," I said, smiling. Hanson swallowed, looking at me. He took a gulp of hot coffee and swallowed again, still trying to get the bite down.

"You're a mean dude," he said. "Trying to scare an old man."

I shrugged. Dave Hartley and Janet came in, saving me from having to come up with some witty comeback.

"You should drop by," he said to Valerie, and indirectly to me. "I'm doing a piece from one of Randy's photos, of the rocks and cliffs as seen from the boat. I usually like the light a little lower, you know, with more subtle, warmer tones, but it's coming out pretty nice."

"Nicely," Janet corrected. "He was going to put a dead body in it. I told him that was insensitive."

"It's art," Hartley said. "Edgy, mysterious, with something to say about how fragile life is, and how easy it is to lose."

"It was insensitive," Janet repeated. "Besides, none of the others are edgy and mysterious. No dentist or doctor is going to want a picture of a dead body in his office."

"True art is never appreciated in one's lifetime. At least not by a wife," Hartley said. He laughed at his own joke, then grabbed a danish.

Jill came in with the breakfast tray, and talk died down as mouths filled.

"A woman with kids," I said, finishing my last bite. "When is the best time for an unannounced visit?"

Janet looked up. "Never."

There was laughter at that. "Seriously, this is not a conversation I can start with a phone call. I need to be face-to-face from the start. How early would she be up and ready, before getting busy doing whatever it is she does on a Saturday morning?"

Gina could not help herself. "If she's got kids, she's already up and dressed. If you want to catch her before soccer practice, you should get a move on. Offer to help with the dishes."

"Who's the lady?" Hanson asked.

Valerie answered quickly. "Catherine Barnett."

"Oh shit," said Hartley. The rest of the table seemed to agree with him. "Good luck on that one."

I stood up. "Yeah, I know." I pushed my chair back in, and left the room.

I went back to pick up my gun, feeling foolish. But I'd rather feel foolish than feel dead. Catherine Barnett was not a suspect in any of the murders, but I'd really hate to explain to Silvia that I'd been shot, again, by a pretty woman, again. At least I expected her to be pretty.

I put the laptop on the car seat next to me and entered Barnett's address in the GPS program. I may have been hoping it was far away, helping to postpone this task, but it was barely 8 miles down the road. I recognized Gill Barnett's car in the driveway, and pulled up next to it.

Catherine Barnett was at the kitchen window watching my approach to the front door. I could see her saying something to someone, probably the kids at the breakfast table. She put something down in the sink and dried her hands to come to the door. I didn't have to knock. The door opened and I was facing the woman whose husband I had found on the rocks at low tide.

"Catherine Barnett?" I said, a little hesitant.

"Can I help you?" she replied, still wiping her hands on a dishtowel.

"I'm Jimmy Davis," I said, handing her my card. "I'm the one who found your husband. I was wondering if I could talk with you for a few minutes?"

She stood there in the doorway, looking at me, and then looking at the card. She considered her answer for a long time. I began to feel even more uncomfortable. I could hear children slurping cold cereal and banging spoons, making tractor noises.

"Come on in," she finally said. Inside my head, I did a victory dance. One small step for a man.

"Drink your orange juice," she said as she led me past the kitchen into a small living room. There was a recliner facing a television, and a small couch. She moved a crocheted pillow from the couch, and indicated I should sit down. She sat down at the other end of the couch.

"I really don't want to bother you," I said, "But I've been trying to make sense of it. It, it hits you pretty hard, finding someone like that, and I'm trying to put the pieces together, trying to help out in any way I can. If this is a bad time, I can come back, it's just..."

"This is as good a time as we're going to get, I'm afraid," she said, trying to help me out. "What would you like to say?"

I put in a dramatic pause. "Do you know a woman named Penelope Dixon?"

She smiled, and relaxed, leaning back on the armrest.

"I think I know what's troubling you, Mr. Davis," she said, looking at my card again.

"You know her then?" I asked.

"I know all about Penny and Gill. I've known for a long time, and we all had a chance to talk it through before, well, before." She picked up the pillow and ran her fingers along the stitching.

I waited. She clearly wasn't finished.

"It's not like it hasn't happened before. Gill is, Gill was an impulsive man. But I knew he'd always be there in the morning. He always was. I know he loved me, loved the kids."

She spoke about her late husband without any tears. I contrasted this in my mind with Daphne Colter, who had more time to get used to her loss. Catherine Barnett was keeping a very tight lid on her emotions.

"You said you all talked. You met with Penny and talked about..." I had no idea how to finish that sentence without doing harm to the fragile rapport I was building.

"I could tell something was really bothering Gill. I figured it had to be guilt over the business with Penny, so I went to see her. That was Saturday. It turns out that he had broken it off with her on the Thursday before that, which is when he started acting funny. She must have said something to him, because on Sunday he comes to me and says he's done something awful and he's all upset, and I told him it was Ok, that I knew all about it, and I knew he would never hurt the kids or me."

I had been an investigator for a long time, and this sounded too much like a cooked story for me to let it go. She was giving a timeline without hesitation. She was not pausing in the delivery. She had thought about what she was going to say. But she could not have been expecting me. Whom had she been rehearsing for? How much of the story could I trust, and what was she trying to gloss over?

Penny had not mentioned a meeting with Catherine Barnett. That would have been an emotional event. Penny did not want me to know about the affair, or did not want me to know about meeting with Catherine. But people don't generally discuss such things with strangers. Maybe I was making too much of it. Catherine, on the other hand, was telling a perfect stranger a whole lot of personal detail. She wanted this timeline on record.

I could play on that. See what else she was desperate to have the world know. "Did Lee Aleada question Gill about Danny McDougal's death?" I asked.

She considered this for a long time. "Pretty much since the day he came here. He was a bully about it." That answer should not have required so much careful thought.

"Did Aleada know about Gill's prison record?" I asked.

"Gill mentioned it to him," she said. "He came by on Friday morning, when Gill was about to take the kids to school. They got really mad at each other. Gill didn't want to talk about any of that stuff around the kids. They both ended up shouting at each other."

"Friday morning?" I asked. "The day he was shot?"

"Gill didn't kill that man," she said calmly, keeping her voice low. The children were still playing loudly in the kitchen, but neither of us wanted them involved in this conversation.

"When did Gill come home that night?" I asked.

"He was in bed when I woke up. He stays out late with his friends on Friday nights. I don't stay up."

"You aren't providing him with an alibi, you realize," I said.

"I don't think he needs one at this point," she said. "Do you?"

I glanced down at her shoes. The shoes of a fisherman's wife, of a mother with two kids. Cheap canvas topped rubber soled shoes. Catherine was a tall woman, and she wore large shoes.

"Can you think of a reason why Penny Dixon would have been at Pelican Point the night Gill died?" I asked.

Finally, some genuine surprise. Followed by a quick stone face, a perfect poker face. She then went back to surprise, or mild curiosity, putting her hand to her chin. "Did she say she was there with him that night?"

I didn't want to answer that question. Let it hang in the air for a while. "Was there anything unfinished between them?" I asked.

"I was nice to her when we talked. She was a little upset, and embarrassed to be talking to me about it, but I wasn't mean or spiteful. I was very understanding. She's coming to the funeral tomorrow. Did you know? You should come too. It's good for the kids to see a lot of people at their dad's funeral. Let's them know he was special." She ran her hands along the pillow again.

"I meant between Gill and Penny," I said. I was certain I had been clear the first time.

"I wouldn't know. She didn't mention anything when we spoke. Gill didn't mention anything." She seemed calm.

"Mrs. Barnett," I said. "Did Gill own a gun?"

"He's an ex-convict, Mr. Davis," she said. "He doesn't own any guns. We don't have any in the house."

"Do you have any idea why Gill was out on Pelican Point the night he died?" I asked.

"Did he go there to meet Penny Dixon?" she asked, making it a question, not a statement.

"Does he normally go there? Is that a common spot to meet people?" She was having no trouble with my direct questions. She was treating this like a police questioning. Perhaps my ex-police voice was coming out. But she had prepared for a grilling, and she was not resisting, not taking offense, not thinking it strange that I would be asking these questions in this manner.

"Pelican Point? It's a tourist spot. There's room to park, and they take photographs of the cliffs, and you can see the waves break right below." She was comfortable talking about the place where her husband died. This wasn't something she was trying to hide.

"Did Gill have any problems with Danny McDougal? Any fights or disagreements?" I asked.

"That insurance guy sure thought so," she said. "He was a real ass about it. Said he had proof that Gill killed Danny. He was a liar. And a bully." She sounded like she was going to say something else, but stopped herself. She studied the pillow in her hands.

"What kind of proof did he say he had?" I asked.

"He didn't have anything. He was making it all up. Trying to get a reaction." She looked up from the pillow, studying my face. I put on my interested face.

"Did he get a reaction?" I asked.

"Well, they sure ended up shouting at each other. He said he could put Gill away for life. He shouted it in front of the kids."

"On Friday morning," I said.

"Yes. He was taking them to school."

"Why are you so certain that Aleada had no proof?" I asked.

She leaned closer, so she could speak in a low tone without being overheard from the kitchen. "Because Gill was with *her* that night."

"What if I told you Danny McDougal probably died early in the evening?" I asked. "After Gill's friend Rafe Gonzales had a fistfight with him? Penny would have been singing at the time."

"You're saying Gill and Rafe followed Danny somewhere and put a bag over his head?" she asked.

"Is that the way Aleada told the story?"

"Yeah. But he thought it was after midnight," she said.

"McDougal was going to the birthday party of a four-year-old," I said. "They waited until his duties at the lodge were done, and Abigail took her shift at the bar. But four-year-old kids have early bedtimes."

She said nothing. She seemed to be trying to calculate, to find out if this new information was dangerous.

I continued. "Rafe had been really tying one on that night. Apparently had his limit already, before the band had barely begun. Was Gill also drinking heavily that night?"

"What night was that?" she asked.

"September 29th. A Monday."

She considered. "He came home late. I could always tell when he'd been with her, he'd come home late. I'd pretend to be asleep. I don't know if he was drunk. He smelled like beer, but they always stop for a beer after they get the boat in."

"So Aleada could have been right," I said.

"He had no proof," she insisted. "He was bullying Gill. That was all."

It was time to back off, so I opened up the conversation. "Was Lee Aleada bullying other people? Were there others who might have had a grievance with him?"

"I bet just about everyone he talked to. He wanted everybody to think *they* were a suspect. He was rude, he was mean, and he would lie to people. I doubt anyone who met him would cry at his funeral." Her face lost expression again, turning from hateful to bland in an instant. I began to think she blamed Aleada for her husband's death somehow. Had he killed Aleada, and then committed suicide rather than go back to prison?

"Do you know anyone who might have had reason to kill your husband?" I asked.

She studied my face again, taking her time with her answer. "You're thinking maybe I pushed him off the cliff? Pissed off that he'd had another affair? Talk to Penny Dixon. It was over. I was Ok with it. I mean, yeah, it hurt, but I won. He stayed with me."

I smiled. "No, I wasn't thinking you. Of course, if you'd known Penny Dixon had met him that night at Pelican Point, then someone might wonder if it was really over between them. But that was the night he died, so you couldn't have known. I suppose you could have found out about it, and killed him the next morning, parking the car there on Pelican Point, and dumping the body in the ocean somewhere nearby, but who would believe such a wild story? The simpler story makes so much more sense."

This time it was Catherine who smiled. "Nice try. We both know I would never kill my children's father. I love Gill. Loved him I mean. And besides, he's twice my size. I'd have to shoot him or something." She was comfortable that the speculation had gone to whether or not she had killed her husband. This was a safe area for her. Something else was not, but I could not see what it was. I'd have to go over the recording. Maybe a few times.

"I agree," I said. "Just getting the wild stories out in the open, so we can shoot them down. But the question was whether you knew anyone *else* who might have wanted him dead. Did he have any enemies? Did he hang around dangerously impulsive people with quick tempers? There's no suicide note, no reason to think he was distraught enough to take his own life. You had settled the thing with Penny. He knew his family loved him. Why is he having a funeral tomorrow?"

She looked at me without saying anything, and then closed her eyes, as if trying to squeeze out a tear that just wasn't ready yet. When she opened them again, there was nothing. "I wish I knew," she said. "I wish I had something to tell the children."

I said nothing at that point. The pause grew. Finally, I stood up. "Thank you very much, Mrs. Barnett," I said. "And yes, I would love to help fill out the crowd tomorrow. I never met Gill, but I feel like I've come to know him. He was a good man. Complicated, but a good man. You and the kids should be proud."

She walked me to the door, past the kids who had stopped playing and had obviously been listening to my final words. I walked out to the car, and as I drove away, I could see Catherine Barnett watching until my car went around the curve in the road.

It didn't take long to get back to the lodge. I went straight to my room, and took off my shoulder holster and stored it away safely in my suitcase. I set up the laptop computer, and downloaded the recordings from my pen recorder into it. For safety, I emailed the files to myself, so they would be safely on a server if something happened to my laptop.

There was one pressing question I needed to know. By now the lab reports should be in. I sent an email to Corcoran, asking if Gill Barnett had been tested for gunshot residue the morning after Lee Aleada's death. And if not, if the body found in the ocean had been tested. GSR is sticky stuff. It can be detected in clothing even after the clothes have been laundered. It might last two days in the ocean, being battered on the rocks. Gill had been found without a shirt. If he had wiped his fingerprints from the gun on his shirt, there would be GSR on the shirt. Too bad that shirt was now just lint in the ocean, after barnacles had removed it from the body.

I played back the recording on the laptop. I could find no fault with the timeline she had presented, however practiced or concocted the story seemed as she told it. The times she had seemed emotional had to do with whether Aleada had any proof that Gill had killed McDougal. Not that he had been a suspect, not that he had been questioned harshly, but that there was no proof. For some reason that was something that Catherine Barnett cared about, something that was important to her. Did she believe her husband had killed the lodge owner? Did that implicate his friend Rafe Gonzales, who was the one who had gotten into the fight?

If she had found her husband was still seeing Penny Dixon, perhaps at Pelican Point, would she become angry enough to kill him? She had talked about winning. Maybe it wasn't about love or jealousy.

Maybe she could not handle the idea of losing her husband to the pretty little redhead. She had obviously been quite pretty when she was younger. She was attractive still, although she no longer put effort into it.

She could have killed him and dumped the body, as late as moments before she called saying he was missing. The time of death after two days in the ocean was going to be hard to pin down. She could even have driven the car back up to Pelican Point. Her footprints would have been obliterated by the deputy sheriff's. But when I had suggested that scenario, she hadn't flinched. Had she expected it?

By lunchtime, I had pretty much given up making sense of it. Maybe there was something in the water up here that made everyone seem guilty. Not that I had seen a lot of water drinkers. But I had been spending a lot of time in bars.

Despite that realization, I walked down the stairs and across the path to the bar, but just to grab a bite to eat. Jill Tarrington was behind the bar, talking to Valerie, who was swiveling back and forth on a barstool. She saw me and waved.

"Hey Jimmy," Valerie said, stopping the chair when it faced me. "How did it go with the widow?"

"I got invited to the funeral," I said. "Tomorrow sometime."

"Eleven a.m.," Jill said. "Everybody's invited. She wants the whole town to come."

"What town would that be?" I asked.

"It's just an expression. She wants everyone she knows to be there, and everyone who knew Gill. She put the word out."

Valerie looked over at me. "You're going to need a suit. And I didn't bring anything black. Looks like *we're* going shopping."

I changed the subject. "Where's Abby?"

Valerie pointed to the ceiling. "Upstairs. Practicing accounting. She didn't want me watching over her shoulder, made her feel nervous. She's entering in receipts, paying bills, all of that stuff. I made her a check list and instructions, and she's just going to town."

"What town would that be?" Jill asked. Valerie made a punching motion in her direction.

I ordered a sandwich, and Valerie had Jill heat up a slice of quiche.

"So," said Valerie, when Jill was busy, "Did you learn anything?"

"She's hiding something. Hell, everybody's hiding something. Except Johnny Mac, he seems to be out of the closet these days. That may be the only thing I've accomplished the whole time I've been here."

"What did she say?" Valerie asked, not satisfied with my vague dodge.

"She was evasive about Aleada. Kept saying he had no proof that Gill killed Danny, but that he had claimed to. That was really important to her. Not whether Gill did it, but that Aleada said he had proof, but didn't have any. But I couldn't get her to say why she was sure of that. She as much as told me Gill did it. She could have said he was with her in bed, but she made sure I knew he was out, presumably with Penny Dixon."

Jill brought over the quiche, and went back to making my sandwich.

"She knew about Penny?" Valerie almost whispered.

"She had a whole timeline prepared. Gill had broken off the affair on the Thursday the 9th; two days after Aleada got here and started asking questions Gill couldn't answer without the affair becoming public. She says Gill was acting weird for the next few days, so she went to talk to Penny, since she had known about the affair for a while. She said it wasn't the first time Gill had done something like that, but she always forgave him. So she talks to Penny on

Saturday, and on Sunday Gill comes home and says he's done something awful, and she forgives him again."

Valerie raised an eyebrow. "But Lee Aleada was killed on Friday night. He could have been talking about that instead of the affair."

I nodded. "She was well aware of that when she was talking to me. She knew I'd see that right away, but she was pretending to be talking only about the affair. She was like that through the whole interview, dodging around, saying one thing, but making damn sure I'd hear the other."

My sandwich came, and Jill found some polishing to do at the other end of the bar, close enough to listen, but far enough away that she could pretend not to hear. If she had some insight, I was hoping she'd come forward with some bit of information that could help. The more the 'town' gossiped, the more I could learn.

"So I make up a wild theory that she killed Gill because he went back to Penny, and then dumped his body in the water and drove the car to Pelican Point before reporting him missing. She didn't bat an eye. She pointed out obvious flaws in the theory and invited me to the funeral. Like she had rehearsed all the possibilities, and she was practicing on me for when the sheriff came along, or for a court case. We might as well have been playing checkers. She was unemotional, except where Aleada's proof was involved."

The big door opened to the bar, and a deliveryman wheeled in a hand truck with boxes labeled "Union Ice Company". Jill jumped up to help him wheel the hand truck through the bar gate and place bags of ice and boxes of dry ice into the freezer compartments built into the bar next to the sink.

Valerie was still trying to connect dots. "So her husband is having an affair in a small town, or community I guess, where everyone knows everyone else's business. She lets it go on for a while, and then confronts the adulteress *after* her husband has broken it off, because he's feeling bad about it. Or about something. That just doesn't sound like how a woman would behave."

Jill, collecting the invoice from the delivery, turned to face us. "It sounds like Catherine, though. She knew Gill liked the ladies when she married him. But as long as he was home in the morning to take the kids to school, she was Ok with it. I mean, they didn't have one of those open things, but she never flew off the handle. She never gets pissed off. She thinks about things. She's a thinker."

The opposite of the impulsive Gill Barnett. She had nothing to gain by killing her husband. On a fisherman's pay, it was unlikely they had any life insurance. There was no other man waiting in the wings to support her and the kids. And she was not prone to sudden homicidal urges. She was a thinker. It was unlikely that she had killed her husband.

But the wild theory I had brought up with her might still have some elements worth investigating. What if Gill Barnett had not fallen onto the rocks under Pelican Point? What if someone had dumped his body in the water, and placed the car above on the cliff to make it look like a suicide? Who had a reason to kill Gill Barnett? Besides the jilted lover, who had carefully avoided letting me know about the affair *and* the visit from Catherine Barnett. Did she really think I wouldn't find out? When everyone in the community seemed to know about it?

I finished the last of my sandwich. Valerie had finished her quiche long ago. "Fort Bragg?" she said as I drained my water glass.

"What about it?" I asked.

"To get you a suit. For the funeral. You're not going dressed like that." She indicated my blue jeans and T-shirt.

I resigned myself to an afternoon of shopping. As I drove the Camry, Valerie in the passenger seat discarding all my presets on the radio, I kept an eye on the cliffside, looking for good places to dump a body. Places a small person could drag or carry a large person without being seen. It would have to be south of Pelican Point, and north of the rock traps we had found the body in. That stretch of coast was only about four miles long. A hike I could manage, especially if I was going slowly, looking for evidence of a body dump.

Valerie had the laptop open in her lap, connected to the cell phone, and was finding men's clothing stores in and around Fort Bragg. I remembered the headache I had developed in the limousine on the way to Russian Cove, and I tried to straighten out the curves as much as I could. Country and Western music leaked out of the radio like something I'd have to clean off the carpet later, but I left the radio station where Valerie had set it. I may be a bachelor, but I was married once.

For me, shopping for clothes is something to get over with quickly. I would have picked the J. C. Penney's, but Valerie had found a small men's clothing shop, and we stopped there. An off-the-rack sport coat was a quick pick, but the slacks had to be hemmed, so we went shopping for Valerie while we waited. Or at least I waited. I doubt there was a shop left in Fort Bragg that we hadn't at least entered.

Four hundred dollars later, I had a suit in a plastic bag hanging from a hook in the back seat of the Camry. Valerie had spent some unknown amount of money on a black dress, despite having come to Russian Cove dressed for the opera. I drove back south, trying to get a Country and Western earworm out of my head, the radio thankfully silent. Valerie was enjoying the scenery.

I stopped when we got to Pelican Point. "You drive back," I said. "I'm going to walk. If I'm not back by sunset, come find me."

"It's not that far, Jimmy." Valerie took the keys.

"I'll be walking along the edge of the cliff," I said. "But don't worry about me; I have a healthy fear of heights."

She drove off. I studied the ground in the pullout area. The mud was now rock hard, and the footprints of Gill Barnett and the small woman were on their way to becoming fossilized. I confirmed again that there were no signs of a fight, and I stretched out on my stomach, my feet under the guardrail, to see as far as I could down the cliff. No signs of blood on the cliff face, no shredded T-shirt remains. If someone had jumped on purpose, he might have missed all the rocks on the way down, until the sudden stop. If they had been pushed, any evidence had been erased by wind and wet fog.

I got up and walked along the cliff edge, looking for broken plant stems, footprints, drag marks, or any other signs of disturbance. The cliff gradually got lower as I neared the dry creek bed, and I started to find deer and rabbit trails leading down to the rocks.

In the tiny cove made by the stream, I could see some abalone divers getting ready to enter the water. Which trail they had used to get there was unclear, but the sturdy grass and rocks of the trail left no sign of their recent passing. If someone had come here at night, carrying or dragging a body, there would be little to show for it. There had been a full moon on the 13th, so even a flashlight might not have been needed, if the person was a local familiar with the trails. They would want good shoes, though. Not a dancer's heels.

It was slow going, since I was following the shore instead of the road. The road and the shore got further from one another as I traveled, and the occasional deer or diver's trail from the road to the rocks became longer. I paid particular attention to diving spots, because most of the terrain was unsuitable for dumping a body. Getting a body to the water was what the divers were doing, although there was less dragging involved. At least one hoped.

I had to backtrack in many places, as the trail ended up against the cliff or in the ocean. It was perhaps three hours later when I decided to quit. The sun was getting low, the light was getting poor, and I was definitely feeling the exertion. I headed for the road, making a few bad trail choices, wondering if I would be able to see the poison oak plants in the fading light. I came out a few hundred yards from the lodge, and walked the rest of the way on the side of the road.

Candles flickered in grinning pumpkins as I walked through the full parking lot. Cars were parked in the empty lot on the other side of the highway as well. Jill had set up her table in front of the reception desk this time, instead of back by the bar door.

"Jimmy," she called out, waving her hands. I walked over to her table.

A Quiet Place to Die

"Here," she said, handing me a ticket. "I owe you one, remember?"

"Thanks," I said, taking the ticket. All I wanted to do was sit down somewhere. I headed towards the noise.

"Hey Jimmy," Jill called out from behind me. "You might want to dust off. Your butt's got dirt all over it."

I turned towards her, said thanks, and began swatting at my rear, generating a cloud of dust. I had fallen on that part of my anatomy several times in the last three hours.

The bar was crowded again, even though the band had yet to set up. There were plastic pumpkins filled with Halloween candy on the tables, and several at the bar. I found Valerie talking to Gina Franco, and handed her my drink ticket.

"How was your walk?" Valerie asked.

"Pointless," I said. "But probably good for me. The best place to dump a body in that whole stretch is Pelican Point itself. I just can't make any case for Gill Barnett not just jumping off himself, and yet there's no reason for him to do that. No suicide note, no deep depression, no nothing."

"Maybe he slipped," Gina said.

"It's possible," I said. "But two murders followed by a fatal accident? I just can't stretch that far. Especially when someone is trying to make Gill out to be a killer, when he has no motive. It is just too convenient. Too coincidental."

"Sometimes coincidences happen," Valerie said.

"Not in my line of work," I said. "Not this time. Everything has to fit. If I can make one of the murders make sense, the others will fall into place. We have all the evidence. It just hasn't fallen together yet."

"So you're out looking for more evidence," Valerie said.

"Yeah. Sometimes something has to hit me in the head three times to make me aware of it."

The band had set up, and Penny Dixon started to play her pennywhistle. I looked over at the singer, dancing lightly on the stage, eyes flashing at the audience below. Was this happy sprite a killer? She'd be at the funeral tomorrow. I had more questions for her. This time I'd get straight answers.

Abigail McDougal was at the bar serving drinks as fast as she could, with help from Maria. Her father had not committed suicide. He was on his way to a birthday party, with a present on the seat beside him. She had no reason to kill him, despite Daphne Colter's insistence. Rafe and Gill had no alibis, but the motive was so weak I could never see putting that theory down seriously in a report.

Rafe and Johnny Mac were sitting at the table at the foot of the stage, along with two muscular men now dressed like their companions in jeans and T-shirts. Of the four fishermen, only Rafe looked up when the twirling skirt belled out. They seemed happy, all of them. Did they share some dark secret? There was no sign of it.

I stayed in the bar until the band quit for the night, studying all the people, staying in the background, and thinking. I went back to my room, still thinking. All of this had started with the death of Danny McDougal. That had to be the key.

§

Penelope Dixon

Blue jays fought a noisy battle for possession of the tree outside my window. I rolled over and put the pillow over my head. Muffled sounds of homicidal birds still made their way into my ears, mixing with the last elements of a strange dream. A pretty lady with a gun was scolding me in raucous high-pitched shrieks. It was Sunday morning, and I had a funeral to attend in a few hours.

Valerie eventually came in and insisted that I start the day with a good breakfast. I told her to start without me. I came down half an hour later, showered and awake, when the sun was well up. Most of the usual breakfast crowd was already there, and I pulled a seat up next to Valerie, and filled my plate with scrambled eggs and sausage from the breakfast tray.

"The whole place is going to just about shut down," she said to me. I had a mouth full of egg, and I didn't reply. "Maria is staying here in case any guests arrive, and to take care of the guests that are already here."

Randy Hanson looked up. "Those guests that aren't going to the funeral, she means."

"Funerals are a waste of time," George Franco said, stuffing a sausage into his mouth. "A bunch of people get up and pretend they liked you, and everybody spends a lot of money putting what you left behind in a place where no good comes of it. When I'm dead, chuck my carcass in the water and let the fish have it. I certainly won't care, and at least the fish will be happy."

"Yes, dear," Gina said. "And don't talk with your mouth full."

After breakfast, I went back to my room to deal with emails that I had been ignoring for days. I wasn't used to having time to kill, but between breakfast and an eleven o'clock funeral, there was no point in starting anything.

At ten thirty, I put on a new dress shirt purchased the day before, and then my shoulder holster. No telling what would happen when all of the suspects in three murders ended up in one room. I put on the slacks, and the new shoes, and finally the jacket. With some adjustment, the gun bulge barely showed.

I knocked on the door to Valerie's room. "Come on in," her voice called through the door. I entered.

"Just in time. Zip me up, will you?" she said, her back to me. The long black dress was unzipped down to a hint of black thong underwear. I pushed below the zipper to hold the dress, pulled up on the zipper, past the black bra strap, and tucked the zipper away between the seams.

She turned around and adjusted the bra with a slight bounce. She looked like she was attending a coronation. The high heels made her four inches taller, and did something interesting to her backside. "Almost ready," she said, checking herself in the mirror, and brushing back a stray bit of coiffure.

She walked slowly on the rough flagstone path to the car, taking care with her heels. The drive to the mortuary was a slow one, as a long line of cars going to the same place was limited by the slowest member.

The parking lot was full, and an attendant in a black suit was directing cars onto the grassy area a few hundred feet from the building. Valerie had to hold onto me and walk on her toes over the grass until we got to the concrete walkway.

Inside the building people were milling about. There were benches for seating, but most of the people were standing and talking. People spilled out into the courtyard on the far side of the room. I saw Penny Dixon standing alone in the courtyard, facing away from the crowd, looking into a small koi pond. I left Valerie to mingle, and went out to stand by the singer.

"I talked with Catherine Barnett yesterday," I said. "Apparently there were a few details you left out when we last spoke."

She turned to face me. "I guess it's no secret anymore."

A Quiet Place to Die

"Why didn't you mention that you were with Gill at Pelican Point the night he died?" I asked, getting straight to the point. There was no telling when all the guests would finish arriving, and when the services would begin.

She looked up at me, wondering how I knew. "That I was the last one to see him alive? After someone was murdered? It didn't seem like the smart thing to talk about."

She didn't seem to be that worried about it now. "Why were you there?" I asked.

"Abby gave me a note. Gill said to meet him at Pelican Point after the show. That's where we used to meet, when we were dating."

That was interesting. I remembered the exchange between Abby and Penny the night I arrived. "Did Abby know what the note said?" I asked.

"It was just a folded piece of paper. Abby knew Gill and I were seeing each other. She didn't approve, but she didn't rat on him."

She looked down at the fish in the water. They were milling around, expecting food to drop at any minute. "But Catherine had already found out by that time anyway," I said.

"Isn't that weird? She came over on Saturday. I didn't know she knew, but when she told me she knew all about it she was just talking like it was something she saw on TV. I would have been mad, but she just wanted to know if Gill was Ok. As if she wanted to make sure I hadn't dumped him. I told her he was just tired of sneaking around, and he couldn't do it anymore. I knew he wasn't going to leave her; he loves those kids too much. Loved them I mean. We were just having fun."

She trailed off, still watching the fish. She dipped a toe in the water, and the fish jumped at the ripples.

"What happened that night at Pelican Point?" I asked.

"He said he had mailed me a letter. It was really important, he said. When I got it, I was supposed to take it straight to the police."

"Did you?"

"No. I still have it at home. I wanted to steam it open and read it first, but it was sealed with tape. I didn't want to give it to anyone if I didn't know what was inside it."

I put my hand on her shoulder. "Penny, did Gill Barnett jump off the cliff at Pelican Point?"

She turned to me, her eyes bright and wet. "I don't know. He was standing by the guardrail, looking out at the water. The moon was full and almost overhead, and it made the water all sparkly. Sometimes we would just sit out there, watching the water together, when there was a moon. He told me to go home. I left. But he was still out there looking at the water."

"You know," I said, as her head fell again to look into the water, "You may have his suicide note unopened back at your house. You really have to get that to deputy Corcoran. Unopened. That's very important. Corcoran has to open it, with witnesses present."

She nodded. "What if he blames me?"

I touched her gently on the arm to get her to look up at me. "He trusted you with the letter. You were the last one he spoke to before he died. He didn't blame you. He trusted you."

She dabbed at her eyes with the collar of her blouse. Valerie came out to join us. I introduced Valerie to Penny. "Could you stay with Penny for a bit? I need to talk to someone for a moment."

I walked away before either of them could speak, and looked around for Abigail McDougal. She was with Jill Tarrington, over by a large arrangement of flowers. I walked over to the pair.

"Jill, could I speak with Abby in private for a moment?" I said, looking at Abby, and gesturing to the door leading into a room not yet full of people. She followed me into a casket showroom. No one else was there.

"I just spoke with Penny Dixon. She said you gave her a note from Gill on Monday night, the night Gill died. Is that correct?"

Abby looked at me, slightly puzzled. "Yeah. You sound upset. Are you upset?"

"No, not at all. I'm just a little excited. Everything's fine," I said. Abby did not seem to be a good judge of other people's emotions, and I wanted to make sure that didn't get in the way. "Did you tell deputy Corcoran about the note?"

"That idiot? He never asked."

"And you never volunteered," I said.

"None of his business. Nobody's business. Gill's got kids. He shouldn't be fooling around. And nobody should know if he is."

"Abby, that could have been important. It could have helped him to find out what happened to Gill." Her eyes would meet mine for a moment, and then find something else to look at.

"It's his job to figure things out. Like that mean insurance guy that kept getting mad at everyone. They're supposed to figure it out. We don't have to do their job for them."

The crowd outside the door became noisier. Catherine Barnett walked through the crowd, and it parted for her. Abby stepped over to see. "First time I've seen her not in her jogging outfit," she said.

"She's a jogger?" I asked.

"I guess. She came in to the bar for lunch, had her backpack on, and she'd been running up the nature trail between the lodge and the cove. She was still sweaty. Had the pot pie."

"How far does she run?" I asked, looking at the trim woman again, with a different perspective. She looked like she had strong legs.

"It's maybe three, four miles to the parking lot at the cove," she said.

"Does she do that a lot?" I asked. "Drop in for lunch after a jog?"

"Just that Friday. Never seen her do it before. Seen her jogging on the road. Gill takes the car, to get the kids to school, and then to get to the boat. She jogs over to the car if she needs it during the day."

"Friday the tenth?" I asked. "The day Lee Aleada was killed?"

"That happened later. She was there for lunch. Pot pie keeps in the freezer forever. We take it out and zap it, then put it in the toaster oven to get brown. It's good that way."

"Were you with her the whole time?" I asked.

"No, the toaster oven is in the kitchen. She didn't mind being all alone though. She's not one of the gabby ones."

The service was about to begin, and Abby and I went in to the main room to get seats. Valerie and Penny were already seated up front. I caught Valerie's eye to let her know she was on her own, and sat down with Abby in the back.

Gill's urn was on a table in front, and a podium stood next to it. George Franco had gotten it pretty close. A bunch of people stood up and said nice things about Gill. Gill's wife and children sat in the front row, and listened. The kids squirmed and fidgeted.

Rafe Gonzales got up and talked about his friend. About fishing for salmon in bad weather. About being best man at Gill's wedding. He broke down a few times, dabbing at his eyes with his sleeve. It was uncomfortable to watch. The big man was not used to public displays of emotion when he was sober.

I could see suited attendants arranging tables with coffee and cookies out in the courtyard. The service was long, and the benches were hard. I began shifting in my seat, and feeling very sorry for the kids, until I saw that they had fallen asleep.

When the service was over, about two thirds of the guests left for the parking lot, and the remainder milled around the main room, or went into the courtyard for coffee and cookies. I found Rafe Gonzales next to a plate of shortbread.

"That was real good," I said, taking a cookie for myself. "He had good friends."

Rafe nodded, the shortbread having absorbed all the moisture in his mouth.

"That night fishing story you and Johnny told Lee Aleada. What really happened that night?" I waited while Rafe got enough saliva in his mouth to speak.

"Doesn't matter now, does it?" Rafe said. "Johnny Mac was at Hartley's. I didn't know it, but when Johnny said we were fishing together, I backed him up. That guy was digging into Johnny's private life, and Johnny wasn't ready for that not to be private anymore. Like I said, don't matter anymore."

"Because Johnny is out of the closet?" I asked.

"He didn't think Gill and I knew. He thought we'd throw him off the boat if we knew."

"When did you find out?" I was still holding the cookie in my hand. I looked for a cup to get some coffee.

"The moment he walked on the boat. We both knew he was a fag from day one. But he seemed to want to go all don't ask don't tell, so we just forgot about it. Except for when Penny started singing at the bar. She wears this tiny little thong thing under that skirt, the same color as her hair, so you think you're getting the real view when it's just undies. Gill thought it was real funny sitting Johnny up there, because Johnny never even looked up. Not gonna tell that story up there in front of the missus and the whole world." He gave a weak laugh at the last sentence.

"So Johnny was at Hartleys, you were shit-faced, where was Gill?" I asked.

Gonzales leaned his head in the direction of Penny Dixon. "Laying pipe in a Miata up on Hill Road. Submarine races."

"Tight squeeze," I said, thinking of how two people could have sex in a Miata.

"She is a tiny one," Rafe said, misinterpreting my remark.

I filled a cup with coffee, and took a bit of the cookie, followed by a slurp of warm liquid of dubious pedigree. Valerie came up next to me, and Rafe moved on to find something to drink.

"Getting anywhere?" she asked.

"I think I know how and when Gill Barnett got McDougal's gun," I said. "I can't prove it, but I'm pretty sure he sent his wife to get it for him Friday morning."

Valerie looked surprised, then satisfied. "So Gill kills McDougal, Aleada finds out, Gill kills Aleada, and then jumps off the cliff out of guilt. The wife is an accomplice. That's why she was so cagey in the interview."

I shook my head. "Gill didn't kill McDougal."

"Who did?" she asked.

"I have no idea."

"If he didn't kill McDougal, then why kill Aleada?" She had the puzzled look again.

"Aleada said he had proof. Gill was an ex-con. He saw himself going back to prison for something he didn't do. That's a motive. He knows where there is a gun. He sends his wife to go steal it. Then that night, he arranges to meet Aleada in the parking lot down at the cove, where no one will hear the gun go off. He shoots

A Quiet Place to Die

him, wipes the gun down, and leaves it in the car. An ex-con would know to do that, so no one would find the weapon on him."

"Leave the gun, take the cannoli. Everybody knows that line." She was getting into the spirit.

"But he got away with it. Corcoran didn't have anything on him. I just can't see him jumping off a cliff out of guilt. He would have had to think he was going back to prison. That's the thing that would have made him so afraid he would kill, or kill himself. But he got away with it. Why are we here," I said, waving my hand at the funeral parlor.

The crowd was thinning. People were in line to say goodbyes to the widow and the children, who were now awake and not very good at standing still beside their mother. Valerie and I got in line.

"Excellent service," I said when it was my turn in front of Catherine Barnett. "A lot of people loved Gill." She said thanks, and turned to Valerie, who just nodded and followed me out the door. She took off her shoes as soon as we got to the grass.

Back at the lodge, I went to my room. There was an email waiting for me, from Corcoran. Again, no message, just an attachment. The lab report on the gunshot residue test that had been done on Gill Barnett the morning after Aleada was shot. Negative. Not on his hands, arms, face, or shoes. Nothing.

"Shit!" I shouted. Valerie came in through the door to her room.

"What is it?" she asked.

"Barnett didn't do it," I said. I pointed to the screen.

Valerie read the report. "But couldn't he have worn gloves?"

I shook my head. "There would have been *something*. Nobody is that good unless they were wearing a head-to-toe condom. Even if he had the gun in a plastic bag, something would have gotten on his shoes, or his face."

I pulled out my phone. Valerie sat down. "What are you going to do now?" she asked.

"I have to see a young lady with a letter," I said, finding the record of the call she had made to my phone to set up the interview. I had the phone return that call. I waited as it rang.

"Hello?" Penny's voice said.

"This is Jimmy Davis. Have you called Corcoran about the letter yet?"

"Not yet. I'm not even home yet."

"I'll call him. Shall I have him meet us at your house?"

"You'll be there? I don't like that guy. I don't want to be alone with him in my house."

"I'll be there," I said. "What's the address?"

She gave me the address. I called the sheriff's office. Corcoran wasn't there. I gave the dispatcher the address, and said it was related to a triple homicide the deputy was investigating, and he might not want to be late.

"Can I come too?" Valerie asked.

"You'll be a witness," I said. "When we open Gill Barnett's suicide note."

I didn't straighten out any curves as we drove north to Mendocino. The radio stayed off, and neither of us spoke much for the whole trip, until Valerie started helping me navigate once we got into town. I had almost memorized the streets of Mendocino by now, and it didn't take long to find Penny's house, even with the GPS and the laptop left back at the lodge.

The deputy's car had not yet arrived. We got out of the car and walked up to the door. Penny opened it before we could knock. She was holding the letter. She handed it to me.

The letter had two stamps, as if Gill had wanted to make damn sure it got delivered. The envelope had been sealed the normal way, with the gummed flap, but then he had written "FOR POLICE ONLY" across the flap along the edge, so that if the envelope had been steamed open, the letters would have to be matched carefully when it was resealed. There was transparent tape covering the writing, and sealing the letter redundantly with the gum. Gill had clearly put some thought into this. Something he learned in prison?

I held the envelope up to the light, but I could not make out the contents. I was careful to hold it only by the edges, but Penny had probably been fingering it for days, and who knew how many hands at the post office had been on it. But Gill's DNA would probably be found under the stamp, and along the gummed seal, if there was doubt about authenticity.

I called the sheriff's office. They said Corcoran was on his way. We waited.

When his car pulled up, we were all on the porch waiting for him. I had photographed the letter several times, but I got another shot of it with Corcoran in the background.

"We have Gill Barnett's suicide note," I said as the deputy pulled himself from the car. He walked up the stairs to the porch, and reached out for the letter. I pulled it back quickly.

"Careful," I said. "It's evidence. Handle it by the edges, or with rubber gloves."

Corcoran took the letter out of my hands carefully, holding it the way he had seen me hold it. He seemed puzzled as to how he was going to open it while holding it that way. I produced my pocketknife, slid it into the corner, and carefully slit the envelope. I handed the knife to Valerie, and quickly pulled my camera up to shoot Corcoran shaking the note from the envelope, being very careful to only touch the edges.

He looked around for a place to put the envelope, and then handed it to me instead. He opened the folded paper carefully. We all crowded in to read it.

In simple block letters, it read, "I killed Lee Aleada." It was signed Gill Barnett.

"That's it?" Valerie asked.

"I was hoping for more of an explanation, like maybe why he did it," I said, echoing her disappointment. I shot a photo of the letter.

"We have his signature on the prison release papers," I said. "We can compare the signature. The address is the same kind of writing, mostly block letters but with some cursive connectors, like on the 'L's."

Corcoran slipped the letter back into the envelope and left it in my hands while he went back to his car to get an evidence bag from the trunk.

"So the GSR report was wrong?" Valerie asked.

"It doesn't make sense," I said. "Why would he kill himself?"

Corcoran held the evidence bag in front of me, and I dropped the letter in.

"He just killed two people. It's called remorse," he said, answering my question.

"But the letter only mentions Aleada," I said. "Why kill Aleada if he didn't kill McDougal?" I didn't mention my theory about Aleada's claim of proof. Valerie didn't bring it up either.

"It doesn't say he didn't kill McDougal," Corcoran said. "Of course he killed McDougal. That's why he killed Aleada." He walked back to his car, not thanking us or saying goodbye. He struggled with the seat belt for a while, and then drove off.

"Why would Gill want to kill Danny? He liked Danny," Penny said.

"He didn't kill Danny," I said. "I don't think he killed Aleada either. Something is really messed up here."

We got back in the car and drove back to Russian Cove. There was to be no band playing at the bar tonight, as both Abigail and Penny thought that celebrating on the day of Gill's funeral was not fitting. But Abby, Maria, and Jill were not idle. Halloween decorations were sprouting everywhere, and the bar had been turned into a pumpkin-carving factory, with sheets of plastic over most of the tables. Even some of the guests were carving faces in the vegetables.

Valerie went to her room to change into clothing more suitable for scooping out pumpkin brains. I walked around the grounds of the lodge, trying to piece things together. There was a large swing set on the south lawn, a sandbox, a wooden jungle gym, and a tire swing hanging from the limb of a tree. Wooden stakes made a ladder in the tree leading up to a small wooden platform.

I sat in one of the swings and looked out over the ocean. The light was fading, and the sun was hidden behind clouds at the horizon. The waves sparkled, reminding me of what Penny had said about the full moon on the water at Pelican Point. A romantic spot to Penny. What was it to Gill, besides the place where his last minutes on earth would be spent? A man who lived and worked at sea, what did he see out there?

I stayed out in the playground until the air got chill. Bats were starting to hunt for flying insects. I could see them flit against the fast fading post-sunset sky. The mother raccoon was leading her string of cubs back to the pond. The world was making sense again. All the answers I needed were in a cardboard box.

§

Abigail McDougal

The squabbling of the blue jays seemed somehow pleasant and amusing when I awoke the next day. My week at the lodge had been good for me. Cobwebs of inactivity had been cleared away, and I had a fulfilling sense of accomplishment. I got up and showered, put on a new shirt, my comfortable old jeans, and I was all ready for the new day. Valerie's knock at the door between our rooms came at just the right time.

"You're looking chipper," Valerie said as she caught me starting to whistle an old Disney tune. I opened the door, and the sun was just peeking over the hills in the east. The air was crisp, but not cold, and we walked down to breakfast together.

Gina, George, and Randy were already there, and the breakfast tray was loaded with steaming eggs, bacon, and sausage. A tray of pastries had been attacked already, and half the pile was already gone. I sat down and poured a coffee for Valerie, and then one for myself.

"Where'd you go after the funeral?" Hanson asked. "I was going to catch up with you back here, but you'd already gone."

I put down the steaming cup and reached for a danish. "We were at Penny Dixon's place in Mendocino, opening up Gill Barnett's suicide letter." I took a bit of danish.

Three mouths opened. Gina was the first to speak. "What did it say?"

I swallowed, and Valerie answered. "He said he killed Lee Aleada," she said. "That's all it said."

"The deputy sheriff is probably closing the investigation," I said. "He has all the pieces now. Aleada knew Gill had killed McDougal, and was getting pushy. Gill admits to killing Aleada, and then jumps off a cliff. All neatly packaged just before the election for sheriff."

A Quiet Place to Die

Valerie gave me a look, but I took another bite of danish.

"Interesting week for you then," said George. "Better than writing real estate ads, eh?"

"It's been a delightful week," I said.

After breakfast, I went to find Abigail. I found her in the bar setting up glasses she'd carried in from the kitchen.

"Can we talk for a bit?" I asked. "In private?"

She looked up at me, and then waved at the empty bar. "Looks like it."

I slid into a bar stool and swiveled it to face her. "Did you know you have a four-year-old sister?"

She stopped pulling glasses from the basket. "If I had a sister, wouldn't she be living here?"

"Half sister," I said. "She lives with her mother in Point Arena."

Abigail studied my face, trying to figure out if I was serious. "She should live here. This is the best place in the world to grow up."

She continued to look at my face. She didn't look away as she usually had.

"Her mother is a waitress. Your father changed his will to make sure Sarah was provided for. Sarah is your sister's name. Her mother is Daphne. She says she met you once."

Abby picked up another glass. "I don't remember a Daphne. She should live here. We need a waitress."

I watched her place glasses neatly in precise rows. "She may not want to live here. They'll have enough to live anywhere they like. She thinks you killed your father to keep him from changing the will."

Another glass slid into place. "I didn't kill him. So she could live here. I could have a sister. I could push her on the swings."

"I know you didn't kill him. Do you know where the box is? The one the deputy used to put all his personal effect in? All the stuff from his pockets and from the car?"

She walked over to the end of the bar and opened a low cupboard. "It's right here. It was on the shelf, but someone took the gun out of it, so I put it down here." She took out a cardboard box that said Union Ice Company on it. The bottom of the box was wrinkled where it had gotten wet.

"This box is what killed Danny McDougal," I said. "He took it out of the freezer the night he died. He was taking it to Sarah's birthday party, to make dry ice fog just like he used to do for your birthday parties. But he'd been drinking too much. He fell asleep in the car, and couldn't wake up when the dry ice filled up the car and pushed out all the good air. He didn't have any of the windows down, because of the rain."

She looked at the box, a glass in her hand. "This was his favorite time of year. He loved making the Jack O' Lanterns blow fog out of their mouths. He wanted to die in his sleep. I think he was happy."

I looked at Abby. She wasn't sad. She wasn't wistful, or mourning. She was thoughtful. I didn't think she'd ever really be sad. I hoped she could be happy.

Valerie was waiting by the koi pond when I left the bar.

"You look different today," she said. "More like the Jimmy Davis I used to know. You've figured it out, haven't you?"

I nodded, looking at her. "There's just one more piece to put together," I said. "One thing that needs confirmation."

"And then you'll fill me in?" she asked.

I nodded again, a tiny bit of a smile escaping from the corner of my mouth.

"I like you better like this," she said. "Silvia said you just gave up. You just quit everything, and went looking for a quiet place to die. She couldn't handle that."

I looked at Valerie, wondering if I cared what Silvia thought anymore. "I like me better like this too," I said.

She said nothing. I left her there, staring into the pond at the fish.

I went back to my room. I took the gun and shoulder holster from my suitcase one last time, and fastened it on my shoulder. The shoulder that bore the scar from the last time a pretty lady had aimed a gun. I put the jacket on, and went out to the car.

Catherine Barnett was hanging laundry on the line when I drove up to the little house. I got out of the car and walked up the path to the gate in the little white picket fence. She looked up at me, pinning a small shirt up on the line.

"Did the deputy call you?" I asked.

"About what?" she said, placing another clothespin on the line.

"Penny Dixon received a letter from Gill. It says he killed Lee Aleada."

She put down the basket of clothes and leaned her back against the laundry pole. Her eyes brimmed with tears.

"Did it say anything else?" she asked. A tear ran down her face, and another followed.

"That's all it said. Just the one sentence. Just four words."

She slid down until she was sitting on the lawn, her back against the pole.

"He didn't have to do it. He said jail was no place for someone with kids to raise. But he didn't have to do it."

"Jail is not a place for someone with kids to raise," I agreed.

She looked up at me, wiping tears from her eyes to see better.

"You might want to burn the clothes you were wearing Friday night. Gunshot residue is hard to get out. And don't forget the shoes."

She climbed unsteadily to her feet. I pulled the jacket open, just enough to show the butt of my gun resting in the holster.

"Are you going to arrest me?" she asked.

"That's not my job anymore," I said. "I think detective Corcoran is writing up his report already, and he'd hate to have to come all the way out here and then have to write another one. An insurance investigator killed by an ex-convict. Small minds like tidy answers. I don't think you'll be hearing from the deputy, except as a courtesy. He'll want your vote on November 4th."

I walked back to the car, not actually turning my back on Catherine Barnett. She was a pretty lady, after all.

§

A Quiet Place to Die

Back at the lodge, I packed my suitcase. I was glad to get the gun and holster tucked away again. I carried my suitcase and Valerie's down to her car. She'd follow me while I dropped off the Camry, and then we'd drive back to civilization together.

There was a crowd waiting to see us off. Abigail, Randy, George, Gina, Jill, even Maria were waiting by Valerie's car. I handed Abigail my card. On the back of it, I had written Daphne Colter's name and address. She looked at both sides of the card carefully.

"Are you coming back next year?" she asked. I looked over at Valerie.

"Absolutely," she said. "We'll be here. Maybe long enough to help you celebrate your birthday."

"That would be nice," Abby said. "I'll make a cake. McDougal's favorite. It's got carrots in it, and cream cheese frosting."

About this Book

This part of the book is for my niece Dacey. She always turns to the back of the book to see if she likes the ending before she reads the whole book. Yes, the bad biker dudes who killed Danny McDougal, shot Lee Aleada, and pushed Gill Barnett off the cliff all got what was coming to them. Jimmy Davis married Valerie and changed the ring tone for his ex-wife Silvia on his cell phone to something polite. The deputy sheriff loses the election by a landslide to the incumbent, and Sarah Colter comes to live with her sister, and plays on the swings and climbs in the treehouse. And all the raccoon babies grow up to be perfect thieves of graham crackers, chocolate, and marshmallows left out by campers on the beach. And the dragon that comes out of the sea in the middle of the book never actually eats anyone, just scares off the bad guys.